Free Rein Series

In Pursuit of a Horse

D1615266

Christine Meunier

Free Rein Series
In Pursuit of a Horse

by Christine Meunier

National Library of Australia Cataloguing-in-Publication Data

Meunier, Christine

In Pursuit of a Horse

1st ed. 2013

ISBN – 978-0-9875332-3-4 (pbk.)

Cover design by Metuschaël and Christine Meunier
Cover photo by Cait O'Pray with thanks to Blinkbonnie Equestrian Centre

Foreword

Whilst working to promote my first novel that was released in July 2013, I had been pondering the idea of writing a horse series for pre-teens. I wanted to be able to combine my love of horses and my faith in a series that would encourage and teach younger readers.

In Pursuit of a Horse follows on from the first in this series, *New Beginnings*. It is my hope that this novel explores the joys of learning about caring for horses.

I pray this series will be a source of entertainment, encouragement and enlightenment for many readers in the years to come.

Christine

Free Rein Series

Also by Christine Meunier

Horse Country – A World of Horses

B and B

The Thoroughbred Breeders Series

Free Rein: In Pursuit of a Horse

One

Jacqui King was excited. Along with two of her closest friends Geordie Smith and Hannah Johnston, the eleven year old was on an adventure.

It had all started out a few months ago, when Hannah Johnston had stated that her parents were willing to buy her a pony for her birthday in February. It turned out that Hannah had an aunt who bred ponies for a living. Hannah's aunt Jan had invited her to come for a visit after Christmas to try out a few ponies and find one that appealed to her.

When Hannah had explained about her horse crazy friends, the invitation had been extended to them. There were five girls in all, but Amelia and Caitlin hadn't been able to come out for the whole trip.

Their families had planned some time away over the summer holidays. Thankfully, the parents of Amelia and Caitlin had promised that their girls could visit Hannah's aunt's place for the last few days that the other girls were there.

Aunt Jan lived a few hours away. Jacqui was glad that her parents were coming along to check out where she would be staying for the next two weeks. She looked out of the back window of the car that she was in with Geordie and Hannah and waved to her parents following behind.

1

The three girls were in a car that Hannah's parents were driving. Kate and Tony – Jacqui's parents – were following Hannah's parents to the 50 acre property in North East Victoria.

The drive took them about 3 hours. Jacqui didn't even notice the long time they spent on the road – she was too busy talking excitedly with her friends about how many different ponies they would try out.

Jacqui was a romantic and thought that Hannah would try one pony, fall in love and decide that it was the pony for her. Hannah stated realistically that even if she loved the first one she rode, she should try out a few to find the pony that best suited her. Geordie thought she should try them all!

The girls were still debating this as the four wheel drive they were in indicated and turned right down a dirt driveway. Jacqui strained against the window, eager to see the ponies as soon as possible.

Jacqui's mother Kate was doing the same while her husband Tony drove slowly down the driveway.

"Look at those trees, honey! I wonder if we should plant trees either side of our driveway. They look wonderful," Kate stated dreamily, causing her husband to laugh.

"If we plant something deciduous then they can provide shade in summer months and let the sun through to the paddocks over winter," Tony replied practically.

"I love it! Will we stop by a nursery on our way home?" Kate asked, her mind made up.

Tony laughed again.

2

"I shouldn't make suggestions that agree with yours unless I'm willing to act them out!" he joked, causing his wife to smile at him.

"That's true! This place looks well maintained. I wonder if Hannah's aunt makes her sole income through the horses on this property…"

"Uh oh… I think I can guess where this is going," Tony stated in mock alarm.

"I didn't say anything about working from home full time through our agistment property," Kate protested, smiling.

"You just did!" Tony retaliated, earning a light slap from her on his arm.

The car pulled up beside the Johnston's in a little area that was marked out by some low lying logs. Tony smiled as he recognised his wife looking in interest, meaning that she was thinking they should do the same for their property.

It didn't take long for the Kings to decide that they were content with their daughter staying a couple of weeks on the property. Jan Somers was a delightful character who, in spite of not having any children of her own, was obviously a natural with them.

Within the first half hour of the families having arrived, she'd shown the girls the room that they would share, had detailed her ground rules and explained that the most important ones were that they were safe and had fun! She proudly showed the Kings around the property, pointing out adjustments she'd made over the years.

Kate and Tony were impressed and told her as much. Jan said goodbye to the two sets of parents when they were ready to leave, waving them off with her three new companions.

"So! Who's ready to meet the horses?" Jan asked in a businesslike manner.

Three excited girls exclaimed yes very quickly. Jan laughed and led the way to one of her closer paddocks. The four stood at the gate as she pointed out the four ponies that lived here. Jan described their colours and markings first so that the girls knew which she was talking about. Then she detailed their personalities, ages and gender.

Jacqui loved that she knew each one individually and was able to provide so much information about them. She decided she wanted to be able to do this with any horses that were agisted at their property Genesis.

The group moved on to the next paddock as Jan led the way. This one housed six ponies and again the girls were introduced to each one.

Jan also showed the girls the two stallions that she had on the property and used to breed her mares to each year. She explained that she kept her broodmares – the ones she used for breeding – separate from the riding ponies that she introduced to saddle and then sold on to other people.

Jacqui loved the set up of the whole property and excitedly talked about this with Hannah and Geordie that night as they lay in bed. Hannah knew her aunt's place well but it had been a little while since she had visited and she was just as excited about this adventure as her two friends were.

They discussed in the dark of their room that night which ponies they would try out first. Jacqui had a dream of owning a little grey pony so she'd chosen one of the two grey horses to ride first.

Geordie had chosen a little chestnut mare that reminded her of the horse she rode at the East Riding School where she had lessons. Hannah hadn't minded which horse she rode first, so had asked her aunt if she could recommend one.

Jan had pointed out that the six horses in the second paddock she'd shown to them were all between the ages of six and ten and that they were all fairly quiet. She said she'd be happy with the girls riding any. She'd obliged Hannah however, and pointed out a little bay pony for her to try first.

Excited about their ride the next morning, the three fell asleep talking of all the ponies they'd been introduced to that afternoon. Jacqui managed to thank God for this time with her friends and riding horses before she succumbed to slumber.

Kate and Tony had checked in with their son Ross as they made their way back to Melbourne. When he reported over the phone that all was well on their property and that he was fine, they had decided they could afford to stop off at a local garden store.

They found some claret ash trees that were full of dark green foliage and about six feet high. Kate could already envisage their beautiful autumn display of dark red and orange leaves. She remarked to her husband that it was a good thing that the trees were plentiful and well priced.

Kate was all too aware that they were investing in someone else's property. She would love to own something like Genesis but recognised that leasing such a property was an affordable way that they could do it for the time being.

Originally when they'd moved to Victoria because of Tony's job transfer, they'd discussed the idea of getting land. Because the transfer involved a three month trial and they didn't have a deposit put away, they'd decided it would be more viable financially to rent or lease a property.

When Kate had found Genesis, she'd talked with her husband about her dream to turn it into a property where they could offer paddocks for rent to horse owners. Tony had felt the idea had merit and the two had prayerfully put together a business plan.

It was at this stage that Kate had raised her concern for investing funds into someone else's property. After all, Genesis had needed work done initially to be able to make it available as a place to keep other people's horses.

Tony had recognised Kate's concern but pointed out that if they developed the property as a business, at least their costs involved could be tax deductible. This had been reason enough for his wife to consider the money they would need to invest to be worthwhile. Even if they were improving the land that was owned by someone else, they were improving it so that they could make money from the property whilst they leased it.

The husband and wife came home late that afternoon, trees strapped safely into the back of their utility vehicle. Kate set to making dinner while Tony filled Ross in on the drive that they'd taken, as well as the property that Jacqui would be staying at for the next couple of weeks.

It was decided that the three would plant the trees after dinner. While Kate prepared their meal, Ross followed his dad's instructions and took buckets of water out to the driveway area.

As Tony guided him, Ross applied water to either side of the driveway. It was hoped that this would help to make the ground that little bit softer for digging. In the Australian summer months it could get very dry, and the ground could get very hard.

"Did the drive seem terribly long?" Ross asked over dinner, thinking that he was glad he hadn't been on the road for the six hours that his parents had.

Tony shook his head.

"I think because we haven't been out that way before, it was a nice drive. It's a pity things are so dry, though. I'm sure it'll be an even prettier drive in the autumn and spring months," Kate commented, imagining the hills they'd driven past as green and full of growing trees.

"Oh! I nearly forgot. Someone rang earlier today about agistment," Ross said suddenly, gaining Kate's attention.

"Ok. I can call them back in the morning. I don't want to make a habit of returning business calls on a Sunday night. Did they leave their details?"

Ross nodded.

"She did. I explained that we had a round yard, tie up stalls and an arena soon to be put in which she said sounded sufficient. Then she said she had three ponies for her two daughters," Ross screwed up his face in distaste, "she also said that they were *very* expensive ponies and she wanted to know that if she kept them here, that they'd be looked after by someone qualified for the job."

Kate smiled, taking in the information.

"Like I said, I'll call her tomorrow. I hope she feels that someone who had horses as a child and competed, counts as qualified!"

"Speaking of which, when are you going to get back into that?" Tony asked innocently, hiding a smile behind his hand.

Kate looked at her husband in surprise.

"I thought investing in a horse at the moment might be money that we could better spend elsewhere," she commented.

Ross laughed.

"I'm your witness mum – dad just said you can get a horse!"

Tony laughed in response, not arguing with his son. Kate looked at the pair, a smile making its way onto her face. Perhaps she'd better start looking!

"Well if we got one, it would be for all of us. I'll need to make sure he's quiet," she mused to herself, causing Tony to laugh again.

"Well, that's decided!" he joked, returning his attention to his meal.

Two

Jacqui awoke early the next morning, despite having had a long afternoon the day prior. The girls had all left after lunch on the Sunday as Jacqui's family had had church that morning. Geordie had attended with them, something that was happening more frequently. Jacqui was glad to have a friend that was into horses and learning about God.

She lay in bed listening to the unfamiliar sounds of this new house that she was staying in. As she listened, she realised someone was already up and making noises in the kitchen.

She sat up slowly and looked around the room. Geordie and Hannah were still asleep off to her right. *It must be Jan!*

Curious and hungry, Jacqui quickly got out of bed. She was careful not to wake the other two. She changed into some light clothes that would be suitable for the warm weather but also for working around horses. This done, she walked out of the room quietly in her socks.

"Are you always an early riser?" Jan asked curiously as she moved some eggs on the hot pan before her.

Jacqui shook her head and took in a deep breath, appreciating the smell. Her stomach growled, causing Jan to smile.

"I think it's the excitement of being here. I don't want to miss a moment!" she replied, taking a seat at the dining room table as Jan gestured her to do.

"Help yourself to some juice. Brekkie will be ready soon and then we can see if food won't wake up your two mates!" Jan stated cheerfully, sprinkling some salt over the scrambled eggs.

Jacqui peered out of the dining room window as she drank. She hadn't seen the garden behind the house before. It was lit up with the morning sun.

"Those sunflowers are huge! Where did you get them?" she asked curiously, looking to Jan.

"I guess I cheated with those. One of the mixed feeds I give to my ponies has sunflower seeds in it. They're good for the horse's coat. Sometimes the ponies miss a few in their feed as they scatter it about the paddock. They're very messy eaters! But, it means that I get some seeds that I can throw in the garden," Jan replied with a smile.

She pulled a few pieces of toast out of the recently popped toaster, and started spreading some butter.

"Can I help?" Jacqui asked suddenly, realising she shouldn't just be sitting and watching.

Jan smiled.

"Absolutely! How about you butter these pieces while I start serving the eggs onto some plates for us?"

Jacqui nodded, taking over the task that Jan had started.

"So do you like gardening?" Jan asked.

"Yeah! Mum's started a large veggie garden at the property we lease. Originally she said it would be a good way for us to save money on food, but I think now she does it because she really enjoys it. I love seeing seeds turn into something that we can use in the kitchen."

"Did you know that those giant sunflowers will produce lots of seeds for me? That's something I like about planting them, they grow really quickly and later they produce a lot of seeds that I can put back into my horse feeds – or even eat myself!" she replied with a wink as Jacqui looked at her in wonder.

"There. I think breakfast is ready and we should wake those sleepy heads! It'll be easier for them to ride before it gets too hot."

Jacqui needed no further encouragement. She raced back down the hall and jumped on first Geordie, and then Hannah, gaining exclamations of surprise from both. The mention of food and horse riding had the two girls up quickly and getting ready.

Kate hung up the phone with a sigh.

"I guess we didn't just get a new customer?" Ross asked curiously.

Kate shook her head.

"It seems that because I haven't got an industry qualification to demonstrate my knowledge of caring for

11

horses, she isn't interested in keeping her horses here. Oh well. I'd better get off to work honey. I'll be back early afternoon. There's plenty of food in the fridge, make sure you have a decent lunch, give Jack a good walk and don't spend too much time in the sun once it gets really hot!" Kate directed as she picked up her bag and keys.

Ross nodded dutifully, used to his mother's caring rant. He waved her goodbye as he finished his cereal. Looking around the house he grinned. *I have this whole property to myself for awhile! What will I do?*

Thinking about his mother's comment he threw on some runners, grabbed his soccer ball and raced outside to find their young dog. A run around one of the larger paddocks would be great before it got too hot.

Tony had looked into a nearby soccer team for his son at Kate's urging when they'd first arrived at Genesis the year before. Ross really hadn't been happy about the move and leaving all of his friends. Kate had felt that if he was kept busy and given a chance to develop new friends, then this would change. She had been right.

The fact that a teenage girl Ross' age lived next door had also helped things along. Kara and Ross had been out a couple of times and really enjoyed each other's company. The Kings had come to appreciate the down-to-earth girl that was seeing their son, and teaching their youngest to horse ride.

Kara had a horse of her own that she rode in the paddock. She'd taught Jacqui that it wasn't necessary to have a fancy riding arena to learn to ride a horse in.

When Jacqui had first met Kara, she'd been amazed to find that the older girl was willing to invest time in her and teach her to ride. Better yet, she was willing to offer her reliable gelding Banjo as the horse she learnt on!

Jacqui had always been interested in horses, but at that stage hadn't had an opportunity to learn to ride them. She'd been ecstatic when her parents had announced Tony's job transfer and their plan to lease a property where they could keep horses. Of course, the Kings didn't own any horses. Their focus had first been on turning the property into a safe place to keep horses, and then on finding clients who would pay to keep their horses there.

Jacqui had met Hannah and Geordie on her first day at her new school and when they found out she loved horses that had started their friendship. Geordie and Hannah rode regularly at a riding school that was located right next door to where Jacqui lived.

Jacqui was keen to join them in riding lessons, but had found that having one-on-one lessons for free with Kara suited her – and her parents – just fine. She loved riding Banjo and had learnt to walk, trot and canter on him before the girls had been invited to stay at Hannah's aunt Jan's place and try out some of the ponies.

Ross thought about how different life was now. He missed his friends in South Australia, but was glad for the friends that he had at soccer, school and of course Kara. He realised as he threw a stick for Jack to chase, that he was glad that God had offered them a chance to move.

"Plus now we're allowed to have a dog!" he said to Jack, patting the kelpie on the head before throwing the stick again and kicking his soccer ball ahead of him.

For Ross King, life was going well at that point in time. In fact, this seemed to be the case for the whole family.

Jacqui grinned as she trotted along on the little grey pony Prince that Jan had helped to saddle up for her that morning. She was riding in a smaller paddock with Geordie and Hannah also trotting on their ponies. Jan stood in the middle, watching the three.

"Now I know that I said the main points to focus on whilst here are safety and fun, but that doesn't mean that we should stop learning. In fact, learning is fun, especially when it's about horses! So girls, do you each know about trotting diagonals?" she questioned, gaining a nod from the three.

Jacqui suddenly thought that she was glad Kara had taught her what they were and explained why it was important to rise to the pattern of a particular foreleg.

"Great! Now I want you to all look down at the outside front leg of your horse. Are you moving in time with it?"

Jacqui realised she wasn't and so sat two beats of the trot before she started rising again. This changed her diagonal so that she was rising and falling with the outside leg.

"Good job, Jacqui! Now all three of you are on the correct diagonal."

Jan encouraged the three girls to change direction and their trotting diagonal, one at a time. She reminded them about the importance of riding at a safe distance from each other, pointing out that Geordie and Hannah's two ponies sometimes didn't get along.

Geordie and Hannah wanted to jump, expressing this to Jan. With a smile she told them that there would be plenty of time for that in a few days. She wanted them to get to know her ponies first – and for the ponies to get to know the girls! Jacqui liked this idea. She'd done a tiny bit of jumping on Banjo with Kara, but the idea of jumping on a horse she'd only ridden once seemed a bit scary to her.

The girls rode for an hour before cooling out their ponies and wiping them over with a damp sponge. Jan pointed out that now that they'd tended to their ponies, they'd better refresh themselves!

The three were thankful for the fruit and cool drinks that Jan offered them.

"So what are we doing next?" Geordie asked curiously, munching on a piece of watermelon.

Jan grinned.

"How many riding ponies do I have?" she asked a question of her own.

"Umm… six," Geordie replied uncertainly.

"And how many did you three ride this morning?"

"Three!" Hannah responded.

"So how many still need to be worked today?" Jan asked, earning exclamations of surprise.

"We get to ride a second horse? We're riding twice today?" Jacqui asked.

Jan laughed.

"Of course! As much as you three might be having fun, I'm happy to put you to work and my ponies need to be worked regularly! Before it gets too hot, you might as well each try out another horse! Tomorrow you can each ride once, which will give three of them a rest, and then we'll reverse that the following day. How does that sound?"

The three thought it sounded wonderful. Refreshed from their break, they took the head collars and leads offered to them and followed Jan back to the paddock to catch their next mounts.

Geordie wondered aloud if this was what heaven looked like. Hannah nodded, thinking it must be. Jacqui grinned.

"I'm sure it says a lot in my bible about heaven. I'll have to look it up," she mused, putting a head collar on a little brown pony this time.

The girls enjoyed another lesson with Jan teaching them about getting their horses to lengthen their stride at the walk and trot. Jacqui realised after the two riding sessions that none of them had cantered yet. She was surprised to find that she didn't mind at all – she'd been learning so much and enjoying trying out two of the ponies that it hadn't felt like there was time to canter!

They chattered over lunch about the two ponies they'd each ridden. Jacqui couldn't decide which she liked better. They'd both been well behaved ponies and she had really enjoyed herself. Geordie had preferred the second pony that she rode whilst Hannah felt that the first she rode had been a little bit more fun.

The girls were excited to think that they would be riding a different pony the following day.

"I can't believe that in such a short space of time, we will have ridden so many different ponies!" Jacqui stated in wonder, causing Jan to smile as she directed the girls to put their dishes in the sink.

Once they'd done so, she took them outside to a wooden bench that was in the shade of a large tree. Hannah looked around, confused.

"What are we up to?" she asked her aunt.

Jan explained the discussion she'd had with Jacqui that morning about sunflowers.

"I know you will have lots of memories about your stay here, but I wanted to send you home with something concrete to remind you. So! I'm going to give you a pot, some potting mix and a few sunflower seeds each and we're going to do some planting!" she announced.

Geordie seemed unsure at first, but shrugged her shoulders. Jacqui was thrilled. The three got to work filling their pots with potting mix before placing a few seeds in them, spacing them out well. Then they covered them over with some more mix, watered them well and placed them in a shaded spot that Jan said would get sunlight in the morning.

"Just you watch, by the time you three head home, they'll have turned into little seedlings for you to show off," Jan commented as she headed back inside to the cool air conditioned living room.

The three followed, Jacqui thinking how wonderful this would be. She realised too that it would also be sad because it would mean the end of their stay at Jan's.

Three

Jacqui looked at Hannah and Geordie's excited faces, not sure what the current scene meant.

The girls had slept a bit later that morning, due to having tired themselves out from the two rides and the hot weather the day before. Jan had taken advantage of this by bringing in ponies for each of them to ride, and placing gear to the left of each pony.

Jacqui had commented after she'd brushed her pony that the saddles seemed to be missing. She could find the bridle she was supposed to put on but had paused from attempting to do so. She'd noticed the day before that Jan had put the saddle on first and then the bridle. Also, Jacqui wasn't sure about all the straps and buckles on the bridle and how to put this correctly on a horse.

As soon as she mentioned the lack of saddles, Geordie had looked at Hannah excitedly before turning to Jan and asking if they were riding bareback.

"What's bareback?" Jacqui had eventually asked after seeing Jan nod that they would be doing so.

"It means that you ride the horse without a saddle on. It's back is bare," Hannah explained, undoing the noseband on her pony's head collar before putting the bridle on.

Jacqui watched her do this, trying to take it all in as she thought about the idea of riding without a saddle. *How will I get on the horse? Won't the trot be really bouncy? How will I rise without stirrups? Will I look silly?*

So many questions flitted through her head as Jan came over to help her with the bridle. Jacqui followed Jan's directions, smiling in triumph as she managed to put the bridle on by herself under Jan's direction.

"I did it!"

"You did! So I guess you'll be learning at least two new things today," Jan commented with a smile.

Jacqui looked up at her in surprise.

"Two?"

"Well you just put a bridle on by yourself for the first time and now you're going to ride bareback for the first time... am I right?"

Jacqui blushed and nodded her head.

"How will I get on?" she whispered so that Geordie and Hannah wouldn't hear her.

Jan smiled.

"I promise I'll help. I have a mounting block that all of you can use. It'll mean that you're standing on something higher. Plus, Matty here," she patted the little bay pony that Jacqui would be riding, "he's really short and that'll help, too!"

Jacqui smiled. Hannah and Geordie announced that they were ready.

Under Jan's instructions the three girls led their mounts by the reins of the bridle, standing at their shoulder on the left hand side. Jacqui made sure she kept a decent space between her pony and Hannah's that was walking in front.

Jan had explained that some horses didn't like it when others came up too close. If this happened, they might kick out to the other horse to warn it to stay away. Unfortunately for the person leading the horse, they might get kicked unintentionally!

When the three were in the arena again Jan had them line up side by side. She took the mounting block first to Geordie who stood on it and then slid herself onto her pony's back as if it was the most natural thing in the world.

Jacqui watched keenly as Hannah did the same. It looked easy!

Jan then brought the mounting block around to where Jacqui was standing at her pony's shoulder. She placed it right beside Matty.

"Ok! Stand on that for me first. Then you can hold onto a bit of his mane at his wither there and put your right leg over his back. Be careful not to kick him."

Jacqui followed her instructions, grinning proudly as she sat astride Matty without a saddle on. *I did it!*

Her elation quickly turned into concentration as Jan directed them all to walk their ponies around to the right. Jacqui was relieved to find that she didn't immediately fall off. After she'd done a lap in each direction she started to relax.

"That's better. Your pony will feel when you're tense and wonder if there's something he should be scared about too!" Jan commented as she walked beside Jacqui.

Jacqui looked to the older woman and smiled in wonder.

"They're really that sensitive?"

Jan nodded.

"Oh yes! They can feel your emotions very strongly. The more relaxed and confident you are the more relaxed and confident they'll be with you! Speaking of which, have you learnt how to do a sitting trot, Jacqui?"

The young blonde girl nodded.

"Good. When we trot bareback you don't need to worry about rising to the trot. Just ride it as you would for a sitting trot. Does that sound ok?"

Jacqui thought this over and realised it made sense. After all, she didn't have any stirrups! She nodded in response, patting Matty on the neck.

Once Jan was happy that the girls had walked their ponies in both directions and practised stopping and going, she announced that they were going to try out a trot bareback. All three grinned in excitement. Let the fun begin!

Kate hung up the phone a tad disappointed. She sat quietly, looking at the notebook that she'd started keeping for potential clients at Genesis. She'd had one potential customer that sounded like a real possibility that week but they wouldn't have their horse in the area for another month. She knew she couldn't rely on possibilities.

Even genuine agistees like the two horses that they currently had didn't guarantee an income. It was when the money came in each month that the King family could then make use of it, not before.

Kate realised with a start that the three other calls she'd had inquiring about their agistment property that week had in some way or other wanted assurance about her horse husbandry skills. Prompted with an idea, she headed from the kitchen into the office she'd created and started up the computer.

A search online generated immediate results for what she had in mind. Kate knew she had horse experience, but saying so at this point in time wasn't enough for some clients. As the property built up a reputation, that would be a different story. But for now she needed proof of her skills and perhaps gaining a qualification was a way to do this.

The thirty something mother of two decided that it might just be possible for her to go back to study alongside her current job. She got excited about the possibility of gaining a qualification whilst still earning income to support the property and their family. Suddenly she couldn't wait for her husband to get home so that she could run this idea by him.

Kate printed off the details of the few courses she found within Victoria and a couple that she could do online. She had just finished this when Ross came in the door.

"Mum, I'm home!"

"In here!" Kate called out from the office.

Ross appeared at the doorway.

"Are you working?" he questioned sternly, causing his mother to smile.

"Now I thought the rule was that every member of this household would take a day to rest each week. That means that even when I've finished my paying job for the day, I'm allowed to do things for Genesis. But no, I don't believe I was working," she informed him with a grin, ruffling his hair as she headed through the doorway and back out to the kitchen.

"Hungry?"

"Yeah! I had a great jog around the paddock whilst Kara rode Banjo. I don't think she realises that helping me to stay fit is easier on her than it is on me," he joked, pouring himself a glass of juice.

Kate laughed as she put a plate of carrots and celery on the table with a couple of dips. Ross grabbed a few sticks of carrot and started munching.

"I think you might take that comment back when we get a horse," she replied as she sat down opposite him to eat, "it's a lot more physically demanding than it looks! Once you start riding you may argue that you prefer jogging because it's easier."

Ross laughed.

"Doubtful. So have you had a chance to look at any horses for sale?" he asked.

Kate nodded.

"There are actually two geldings at a property an hour from here. I thought we might go on Saturday to take a look if your father wants to. It may be nice to spend a Saturday looking at a potential horse rather than him feeling that he has to do something to add value to this property for our agistees."

Ross nodded. He'd helped his father to build a round yard where horses could be lunged or riders could feel safe first getting on a horse in a smaller area.

Tony had also created post and rail separators to go in a three sided shed that was already on the property when they'd arrived. Now people could use the cover of the shed to put their horses in, tie them up and tack them up.

The pair finished the snack Kate had organised before Ross headed off to his room, agreeing with a roll of his eyes that it would be smart for him to get started on the novel he needed to read for English that year at school. Kate smiled as he headed off, thankful that he'd accepted the suggestion. She stood up from the table thinking that it might be time to start thinking about dinner for the two males in her life.

"Hello?" Jacqui asked into the phone.

She'd just called home and her brother had answered. When Jacqui had finished talking with him, she'd asked to talk to her mother. Ross had said he'd get Kate for her.

"Hi darling. How's your holiday going?" Kate asked, smiling as she heard her daughter on the other line.

"Mum! It's great! I've ridden three ponies so far and today I got to ride bareback – that's riding without a saddle. I haven't cantered yet, but neither have Geordie and Hannah. I'm not sure if Hannah has found her pony to buy yet but of the three I've ridden, little Matty that I got to ride today would be my pick if I was getting to choose a pony. The other two were great – I was so happy to get to ride grey ponies because that's my dream. But Matty... even though he's a bay, he's just so willing to do things and he doesn't get scared by anything and he was really comfortable to ride without a saddle! Maybe when I'm able to get a pony we don't need to worry about buying a saddle mum," Jacqui gushed out, causing Kate to laugh.

"It sounds like you've been busy! How are you girls coping in the heat? Is it as hot up there?"

"Oh we're fine! Jan gets us to ride earlier in the day because she says it's better for us and our ponies. Do you know what she had us doing yesterday afternoon? Because it was too hot to ride any more horses – and we'd already ridden two each anyway – she got us to spend time outside with her in the shade to plant some seeds."

"So what did you plant?"

"Sunflowers because I'd commented that morning on the huge sunflowers she has in her back garden. She said they're really easy to grow and did you know that they're good for the horse's coat? I didn't know they could be horse food! So she's given us each a few seeds and a pot and Jan says that by the time we head back home they will have already sprouted. I can't wait to bring mine home and find a spot in the veggie garden for them!"

Kate smiled.

"That sounds delightful, Jacqui. I'm so glad you're having such a good time. It sounds like Jan is very careful with her horses too."

"She is! And I'm learning so much, mum. Today as well as getting to ride bareback for the first time, she taught me how to put a bridle on. By the time I come home I'll be comfortable enough to tack up a horse by myself, I think! Geordie and Hannah already knew how to do that because of their lessons, but at least I'll be able to help them when they bring their ponies to Genesis."

"That's very true darling. Your father's just gotten in the door. Would you like to talk to him? I'd better check on dinner."

"Sure!"

Kate called Tony over and handed the phone to him before going back to the kitchen. She thanked God that her daughter was having such a wonderful experience away from home. She'd been unsure how Jacqui would cope at her age but was glad to hear that the first two days had been so good.

She smiled as she thought how lovely it would be to have found a horse that would suit all of her family. And how much more wonderful it would be if she managed to do that before her daughter was due back home.

Four

Jacqui wiped some sweat from her face before lifting up the wheelbarrow and pushing it along to where Geordie had created a few piles of manure. The girls had ridden earlier that morning but only once because it was going to be a very hot day.

Jan had insisted that another part of horse care was learning to pick up after them. She'd said that the girls should pick up one paddock after their morning ride, before it got too hot to be outside.

Jacqui was glad she had Geordie and Hannah to help her. She questioned how Jan did this by herself each time. It sure was work to clean up a paddock with six ponies that ate so much!

"I'm not sure I like this bit of owning a horse," Geordie grumped as she started putting her piles into Jacqui's wheelbarrow.

"Maybe not… but if we have to do this at Genesis to keep our horses there for free, then I'm up for it!" Hannah responded logically.

Jacqui's mother had offered the girls agistment in return for them helping out around the property. It had been the bartering agreement that had sealed Geordie being able to get a horse. She had never gotten around the issue of where she would keep her horse and how she would afford to keep it, even if her parents had agreed to purchase one.

"I like that we get to do this whilst the horses are in the paddock," Jacqui commented, patting one of the grey ponies Patrick that she had ridden the first day.

He accepted her stroke along his nose as he sniffed at the wheelbarrow. Finding nothing of interest, he let out a puff of a sigh and walked off.

Jan had told the girls to start with this paddock as the ponies they had been riding were the least likely to bother them whilst they were in the paddock. She had warned the girls however, that they needed to be mindful of where they were in relation to the horses and had indicated that she'd be keeping an eye on them from inside where she was working in the kitchen, preparing lunch.

The thought of lunch made Jacqui's stomach growl rather loudly. Hannah looked at her with raised brows. Geordie giggled.

"It's a good thing we've nearly finished here! I'm as hungry as you. My stomach's just not complaining as loud!"

Jacqui smiled at that comment. They hadn't finished the paddock, but Jan had told them that if they managed to at least fill the wheelbarrow three times and empty it on the manure pile, then they would have done quite a bit of work.

Jacqui wondered what Jan did with the manure and made a note to ask over lunch.

"Well that's it, I'm done!" Hannah announced, putting one last rake full of manure into the wheelbarrow.

Geordie and Jacqui agreed. Jacqui was thankful when Geordie offered to push the wheelbarrow out of the paddock. It sure was heavy once it was full!

Hannah trailed behind the pair, watching the ponies standing in the shade of some tall dark green leafed bushes. She noticed that a couple of the ponies were reaching up high to eat what they could reach.

A smile reached her lips as she realised that the plants were nicely trimmed because the ponies had been eating them.

"I wonder what that plant is?" she pondered aloud, causing Jacqui and Geordie to have a look.

"I don't recognise that one but it sure looks like the ponies like it. I guess Jan will know," Jacqui responded.

The three girls emptied the wheelbarrow and put their rakes away with it on the side of the muck heap. The area where they put the manure had three concrete walls around it and a concrete floor. The rakes and wheelbarrow were found against one of the walls and Jan had said that they could return them there.

Jacqui wondered if this was another thing that her parents should consider putting on their property. She voiced this question to the other two.

"I'm not sure it's necessary," Geordie commented, "at the East Riding School they just have an area where the manure is put but it's not really marked by anything. We just know that if our horse passes manure while we're in the tie up area, that we need to pick it up with a scooper and take it around to the manure pile."

"Doesn't the pile get out of control then?" Jacqui asked, imagining an awful lot of manure.

"Nah, I think some people come and take it... for their gardens I guess. So it's often getting made smaller as people come to collect it."

"Jan's looks a lot neater than the one at the East Riding School though," Hannah commented as she reached the door to the house.

The three took their boots off before making their way inside. Jacqui wondered what was for lunch, manure piles forgotten.

The girls enjoyed salad sandwiches and some cut up fresh fruit that Jan had put out for them. With a smile she asked them which part of the morning they'd preferred.

Geordie looked shocked.

"Is that a serious question?" she asked, "the riding, of course!"

"Actually... I had more fun in the riding lesson, but it was nice to learn another part of looking after horses," Jacqui commented shyly.

Hannah nodded.

"Aunt Jan, what's the big bush that you have growing at the side of the ponies' paddock? It looks like it's good for shade, but two of them were eating it!"

"Oh, they're lucerne trees! The other name for them is tagasaste, I think. They're so common around here that people consider them a pest. They grow really well from seed. I love them though. If ever you're going to have your own property in the future girls, I'd encourage you to consider some lucerne trees. They're good for shade and wind protection and as an added bonus, the horses like to eat them."

Jacqui thought she'd have to tell her mother about the trees when she called her that evening.

The three girls enjoyed some time in the living room over the hotter afternoon hours. Jacqui was reading a novel about a Scottish girl who was riding a gorgeous chestnut Arab mare. She loved picturing herself galloping across a beach with the wind in her face and no one else around. How wonderful that would be!

She only had a little left to read of the book that day and once she'd finished it, she started on a book for school that year. Geordie screwed up her face in disgust when she recognised the book Jacqui had.

"You're reading a school book already?" she questioned in a tone that seemed more like an accusation.

Hannah laughed.

"It doesn't surprise me. But I'm surprised you even recognise the book seeing as school hasn't started yet," she teased Geordie.

Jacqui laughed.

"Well I finished the book I was reading for fun. I'd love to read the next one in the series but I promised mum I'd do a little bit of school work while I was here. You could do the same thing, Geordie. Don't you want to start the year ahead? Would your parents take your horse away if you fell behind in school?"

Geordie looked alarmed at the suggestion.

"They wouldn't surely! I picked up my study habits and results last year. That's what made them agree to get me a pony."

"But I'm sure you need to keep doing well in school to keep the pony," Hannah reasoned logically.

Geordie sighed.

"Well we haven't been shopping for my school books yet. I think we'll be doing that when I get home. So how can I start on something I don't yet have?" she challenged the pair.

Hannah looked beaten. Jacqui considered the idea.

"How about this – you can borrow my book to read each night before we go to bed and I'll start my second horse book. When we have time in the afternoon or after dinner, then I'll read my school book," she reasoned.

Hannah grinned.

"Genius," she exclaimed.

Geordie looked so disappointed that Jacqui started giggling.

"What?" the young red head asked defensively.

"Well, I thought I was helping you with my suggestion, but now you look sad at the solution I've given you. You really don't like school work, huh?"

Geordie shrugged and then grinned.

"I guess not… but if it's the way I can keep the pony that I haven't yet got, I may as well start now."

Jacqui grinned.

"Good! I'll loan you my book tonight."

"Are they still teaching about accountability at church?" Geordie asked suddenly.

She'd attended Sunday school with Jacqui a few times and had enjoyed the theme of personal worth. Jacqui nodded.

"I'm not sure what they'll be covering while we're here though. I'm enjoying learning about how to be a better friend and make good decisions."

The two chattered happily about church and a couple of friends that they had there. Hannah eventually interrupted them.

"I'm not sure about all of this church and God talk. Can we change the subject please?" she asked crossly.

Geordie shrugged and started talking about which pony she'd like her parents to buy for her. Jacqui sat quietly, sad that her beliefs made her friend uncomfortable. She'd been excited when Geordie had agreed to come along to church one morning and further glad when Geordie had seemed to enjoy kids' church and had started making friends with others their age.

She'd thought that maybe this would lead to Hannah considering coming along with them. Jacqui concluded that now it wasn't likely at all.

Kate read earnestly from the computer screen. She'd talked with Jacqui the night before and had been curious to hear about a tree that Jan had on her property.

Kate loved plants in general, but when Jacqui had excitedly told her about Jan's love for the lucerne tree because of its many uses, she'd made a note of the name and determined to research tagasaste once she got home the following day. Having found that the tree seemed to have a lot of validity on a horse farm as fodder as well as a wind break and shade, she decided it would be worth discussing getting some with Tony.

Kate didn't feel that the time was right to invest more in the farm, until they had more money coming in. She'd taken another call that had sounded promising that afternoon. The older woman had an old broodmare that had been retired from breeding and just needed a paddock to spend her days in.

Kate was excited about the idea of such a low key customer. It was great to be able to offer facilities to those who were more avid equestrians. But to have a paying customer who just wanted to know that their retired horse was comfortable and able to graze suited her just fine.

She prayed that this possibility would turn into reality in the very near future. She recognised that until Genesis was producing more income than the three current clients, it wasn't smart to invest a lot more into the property.

Kate did reason however that trees were something that should be put in as soon as possible. This way they had time to establish and grow. She pondered the idea of planting a lot more once the summer heat had disappeared and cooler autumn days were on their way.

As she thought about their future on Genesis, Kate also thought of her children's future in Victoria. Jacqui had said on the phone the night before that Hannah had gotten annoyed with her and Geordie talking about 'God stuff.' It was obvious to Kate that her youngest child was upset about her beliefs offending a friend.

She'd suggested that any time it was on Jacqui's mind, that the young girl pray for God to guide her in her relationship with Hannah. She'd also suggested that Jacqui might like to pray for opportunities to talk more about God with Geordie when Hannah wasn't around to be made uncomfortable.

Jacqui had thanked her mother for the advice before talking with her dad. Kate hoped that Jacqui wouldn't spend too much time being disappointed and she prayed that night with Tony that her daughter would find the following day to be delightful and full of learning more about horses. The pair prayed for Ross too and their work situations before calling it a night.

Five

The weather was a bit cooler the following day for the three girls staying with Hannah's aunt. Jan had told them in the morning that she felt it was cool enough for them to ride twice before lunch. This news was met with three cheers.

Jan had laughed before telling them that she would make them work for it! She'd helped the three to tack up their ponies before letting them have a walk, trot and canter. Then she'd set up some small cross rails for them to jump their ponies over. The three girls had had a ball.

When it was time to switch ponies, Jan had advised them to not put saddles on this time as they were going bareback again. Jacqui excitedly looked forward to trying out another bareback ride.

Jan had them warm up at a walk and trot before getting the girls to line up side by side in the middle of her yarded riding area. She directed them to make sure there was a lot of space between each of their ponies.

With them holding their ponies at a standstill, Jan asked the girls if they'd heard of the game 'around the world'. Geordie and Hannah nodded slowly, indicating that they had. Jacqui shook her head no.

"So would you girls like to tell Jacqui about it?" Jan asked.

"Well we've only done it once in a lesson at the East Riding School," Geordie ventured slowly.

"But what you do is sit normally on your horse with you feet out of the stirrups – if you've got a saddle on your horse, that is. Then you lift a leg over the front of the saddle so that you're sitting sideways on the horse. Then you lift the other leg so that you're sitting facing the back of the horse," Hannah explained, Jacqui listening intently.

"And then you lift a leg again and end up sitting on the other side of the horse before sitting back the correct way. It's pretty much making a full circle whilst on the horse's back in the saddle."

"Correct," Jan responded, asking Hannah to demonstrate.

The young brunette happily did so. Jacqui watched in interest, a little unsure. How was she going to do that?

"Will you hold our ponies one at a time for us to do that?" she asked Jan.

The older woman smiled.

"How about I hold Jasper there for you whilst you try it out? Each of these ponies knows how to stand still so I'm happy for Geordie and Hannah to have a go without me holding them. If you girls don't want to, you're welcome to wait for me to stand at their head for you."

Geordie and Hannah quickly stated that Jan didn't need to hold the ponies for them. They set about proving that they could go 'around the world' in either direction on their mounts. They stated with glee that it was easier without a saddle.

Jacqui tried out the exercise slowly with Jan holding onto Jasper's bridle. Achieving this, she excitedly tried turning in the other direction when Jan suggested it.

After this exercise, Jan set up an obstacle course for the girls and directed them on how to complete it. She set a challenge to see if the girls could complete it within a particular timeframe. What Jacqui found interesting was that Jan set a minimum time they must complete it in. She explained to them that if they did the course quicker than this, then they were rushing and couldn't communicate as effectively with their ponies as a good horseperson should.

Geordie volunteered to go first, Hannah quickly saying that she'd like to go second. Jacqui was more than happy to watch the two more experienced girls go through this obstacle course before she tried it out on Jasper.

She remembered Geordie and Hannah bickering about who could complete jumping courses faster when she'd first met them. Hannah was focused on achieving things quickly; Geordie was more interested in style. It surprised Jacqui now that she was more aware of their personalities.

With Geordie more scattered and Hannah more logical, it appeared that the girls switched when it came to competitive riding. Not surprisingly, Geordie managed the course quite effectively, only struggling a little when she had to walk three steps into a U shaped area and then back out of it.

Hannah achieved the course well, but rushed through it and struggled in the same area because she wanted to go so quickly. Her pony ended up stepping over the last pole that made up the base of the U, meaning that Hannah had to ask him to back over this.

Jan gently reminded Hannah about taking things slowly for the benefit of her horse and herself. Jacqui noted that Hannah seemed a bit annoyed by this.

Then it was Jacqui's turn. She'd had a couple of chances to practice backing up but felt that the U shaped area would be the area that she would find the most difficult. When she finished, Jan congratulated her on taking it slowly and getting through the whole course whilst communicating well with her mount. Jacqui beamed at the compliment.

The girls listened intently when Jan informed them that she would leave the course set up for them to do the following day.

"Let's see how you do on a different horse and having been through the course once already. And now I'm dying to ask," she stated dramatically, grinning at the girls.

The three sat on their mounts, waiting for Jan to finish talking.

"What?" Geordie asked, impatient for a reply.

Hannah and Jacqui nodded in agreement.

"Dying to ask what?" Hannah threw in.

"Well, all three of you girls have ridden the six ponies I have available for sale at the moment. So two questions – do you have a favourite and have you two decided on the one that you want your parents to get you?" she asked, walking with the three back to the tie up area where they would untack and brush down the ponies.

"I love Matty," Jacqui piped up uncharacteristically, causing Jan to smile.

"I think he suits you beautifully! It's a pity that you're not yet in a position to get a horse," she responded thoughtfully.

All three girls nodded in agreement. Geordie looked to Hannah, catching her eye. Hannah grinned.

"I think Jasper is for me," Hannah said of the brown pony that Jacqui was riding back to the tie up area.

Jasper was a 14 hand high pony that was 9 years of age. He was a quiet and willing little gelding, suiting Hannah well. Jan nodded her head in agreement.

"I think he's a great pick for you, Hannah. You're welcome to ride him more often but I think it's still good for you to get the experience of riding the others – and of course they need the exercise!"

Hannah laughed, saying that she would like that as she dismounted and tied up the grey pony Patrick that she'd been riding that time. Jan walked over to where Geordie was taking the saddle off Matty.

"And what about you?" she asked as Geordie put the saddle up on the rail before picking up a body brush.

"You know, I'm not sure yet Jan. On the first day I wasn't so sure about Rose... but I would love a chestnut mare and I think I should give her another go in case I find that I was wrong about my first impression."

Jan smiled.

"Good on you, Geordie. I hope you won't let your desire for having a chestnut mare make you choose her if you find that you don't click. But I like that you'd like to ride her again, I think that's wise."

The girls finished brushing down their ponies before taking them back out to the paddock. Jan directed them to put the gear away in her shed and wipe over the saddles and bridles. She told them that she'd be inside fixing lunch and for them to come in once they were done. The three girls raced toward the shed, eager to be able to get a cool drink and something to eat.

Kate hung up the phone from having talked with Jan. It was good to hear from the older woman how the three girls were going. Jacqui gave Kate a run down each evening, but her mother had been keen to hear from Hannah's aunt about how she was coping with the horse crazy girls.

Jan had put forward an interesting proposition for Kate to discuss with Tony.

The older woman had suggested that they might like to lease one of her ponies for Jacqui to build up her confidence and gain more experience. She detailed the little bay pony that Jacqui had fallen for and explained how well they worked together.

"But Jacqui will grow out of him as soon as she has a growth spurt. That's why I'm suggesting you lease him so that you can hand him back to me when she's too big for him," Jan had explained.

She'd also told Kate that she often had ponies coming along that would be made for sale and that she expected she would have a taller pony that would suit Jacqui for a first pony that she could own. Kate had thanked Jan for her suggestion and advice, promising that she would discuss it with her husband and get back to her.

She'd confirmed the cost of leasing Matty, whether a saddle and bridle would be included and how they'd go about getting him to Genesis. Happy that she had all of the details, Kate determined to speak with her husband that night after he got home from work. It would be lovely to organise a pony for their youngest girl at a time when they may purchase another horse for the whole family.

Clouds gathered that evening in the northeast and the girls were surprised to hear the rumble of thunder after dinner. Jan mentioned that it was expected to be stormy the following day.

"Does that mean we may not be able to ride?" Jacqui asked.

Jan nodded.

"We'll see what the weather does but if there's lightning, I don't want you out there riding and I'm not sure that my ponies would like it either! Also, because the riding area isn't under cover, if it's raining that wouldn't be very pleasant and the footing in the arena might not be so good. We'll see what happens tomorrow."

The girls nodded, each disappointed. That night they talked about the ponies that they'd ridden, comparing notes with each other about the six different personalities. Hannah was excited to have made a choice and the girls talked about how much fun it would be once they had Jasper – and possibly Rose – back at Genesis.

The following day continued in a stormy fashion, with dark clouds throwing rain over the property. The girls watched lightning lighting up the hills on the property across the road as they ate their breakfast.

The rain intensified over the morning, meaning that riding was out of the question for the day.

Jacqui settled down with her school book to read whilst Hannah drew a picture of a horse. Geordie sighed, not impressed.

"We should be doing something! Silly rain," she complained.

Jacqui grinned and threw her book across to where Geordie was sitting in a large armchair.

"I think you should read some more of that! If you can't ride, you might as well be doing something that will help you to keep the pony your parents have promised to buy you."

Geordie grudgingly agreed. Jacqui went to their bedroom to get her horse book to read instead. On her walk back down the hallway she heard the back door open and close.

"Where's Jan gone?" she called out as she made her way through the kitchen.

"She said something about needing to go outside and that we should stay in here. She said she wouldn't be too long," Hannah responded, looking up from her drawing to answer Jacqui.

Jacqui looked out of the kitchen window as she heard a low rumble. *More thunder?* She realised the noise was a truck. Curious, she walked to the window to look out amongst the rain.

Jan was waiting at an area where the truck stopped and a ramp was slowly lowered. Jacqui watched her head up the ramp in the rain. Shortly after she came back down the ramp walking a tall grey pony. Jacqui wished it wasn't raining so much so that she could see things more clearly.

Jan disappeared out of view of the window, causing Jacqui to head back to where Hannah and Geordie were. Geordie seemed focused on the book that she should be reading and Hannah was intent on her picture of a horse jumping a log. Jacqui made a note to ask Jan about the new horse when she came back in.

Six

It wasn't until the following day that Jacqui was able to meet the new horse. She'd asked Jan about it the night before and had been informed that he was a gelding she'd sent away to be started under saddle the year earlier.

The horse named Jaq had come back to Jan last year after his session with a trainer. Jan had loved the gelding from the day of his birth, but admitted to the girls that he was a little bit of a handful.

"He just seems to know how beautiful he is!" she'd joked, causing them to smile.

Jacqui had asked if Jan was going to keep him. She'd responded that he would be like the six ponies that the girls had been riding. She mentioned that it'd be a shame for her to keep him when someone could be out competing on him and winning ribbons.

Hearing how highly Jan spoke of the young gelding, Jacqui fell asleep dreaming of a grey pony galloping across a paddock, his mane and tail streaming in the wind. Jaq was on her mind when she awoke the next morning.

Jacqui lay in bed, listening. When she didn't hear any rain or thunder she tiptoed out of bed and across to the window. Pulling back the curtain to peek out, she was delighted to see blue sky and a bright sun.

"Yes!" she shrieked, causing the two others in the room to stir.

"We'll get to ride today!" she told them, causing Geordie and Hannah to get up quickly and get themselves ready.

Jacqui managed to dress and eat her breakfast before the other two. She hurried them along, thinking about the grey gelding that had arrived the day before.

The three girls headed outside with Jan, talking about which pony they would ride first that day. Geordie and Hannah raced ahead to the tack shed while Jacqui looked around for the new horse.

"Looking for something in particular?" Jan asked, smiling lightly as she thought she already knew.

"Where did Jaq get put yesterday?" Jacqui asked, confirming Jan's thoughts.

"Over this way," she directed, leading Jacqui to a smaller yard that was now occupied by a grey gelding.

Jacqui took in a quick breath when she saw Jaq standing alert, his eye on the two approaching. *He's gorgeous!* From what Jacqui had been learning, Jaq was about 14 hands high, quite a bit taller than little Matty that she was enjoying riding.

"Will he grow much taller?" Jacqui asked Jan, her eyes on the gelding.

"He shouldn't. He's turning six this year so he should have stopped growing. Come on, we'd best see how those two girls are getting on with the tack."

With a sigh Jacqui followed Jan to the tack room. Geordie and Hannah had pulled out three saddles and bridles that were known to fit the three ponies the girls were riding together. Geordie handed a head collar and lead rope to Jacqui.

"Where did you disappear to? It's time to ride!"

"Just to look at Jan's horse that arrived yesterday," Jacqui responded, taking the head collar from her.

"Ok, well let's get these ponies! I want to see how Rose is feeling after all of that rain."

The girls each caught their favourite ponies for the morning ride. Jan directed them through the obstacle course they had been over twice already. She congratulated each of the girls on their improvements through the course whilst riding different ponies. The three girls beamed.

"So what are we doing after this ride?" Hannah asked, curious.

Jan grinned.

"We're going to tack up the other three geldings and I'm going to put a saddle on my old boy Red and we're going on a trail ride!"

Jacqui beamed. Geordie and Hannah looked surprised.

"Really?" Geordie asked with a grin.

Jan nodded, directing the girls to take their ponies to the tie up area to untack.

"Otherwise it'll be lunch time and then it'll be too hot to go out on another ride!" she warned them, causing the three to encourage their mounts to walk quickly back to the area where they could be secured and unsaddled.

Kate sorted through the mail that had been delivered that day. She grinned as she spied a larger envelope with a familiar TAFE logo.

Tony and she had discussed the idea of gaining a horse qualification to help generate more business, or at least to turn potential customers into actual paying clients. They'd done the figures and thankfully, because Kate was living in Victoria and had only completed a qualification up to Certificate III level, this meant that studying a Diploma of Equine Performance Management was a viable option financially.

The course was still going to cost more than the Kings wanted to spend at that point in time. They'd done some figures and realised that if they adjusted their budget a little and paid for the course in instalments, then they should be alright.

Kate had had a lengthy chat with the course coordinator for the Diploma she was considering doing. She was thankful to find that some of her previous horse experience could be taken into account as well as her current agistment business. This meant that for a couple of subjects she would be able to gain a grade very quickly.

The course was going to take her two years to do but could be done via distance education. This meant that Kate could continue to work her job and run the property at home.

She'd just need to set aside time each evening to fit in her necessary reading and assessment items.

This dealt with; Tony had suggested that Kate might as well find out about enrolling for the new year as soon as she could. The papers that had come in the mail were just those; papers she needed to sign to be enrolled into the course.

Kate quickly filled in the necessary details before putting them into a reply paid envelope. This done, she told Ross she was going into town to post something and promptly headed off. She thought how wonderful it would be to tell potential clients that she was undertaking a Diploma of Equine Performance.

"That should gain their attention," she murmured determinedly, driving slowly down the driveway.

She smiled at the sight of the young trees either side of the drive that Tony and Ross had helped to plant. The property was improving little by little and Kate loved that they were making the changes to help it look better and be more functional as a business.

"Now we just need to be able to purchase Genesis, God. I can't imagine how much they'd want for this property."

Kate knew it would be a long time before they had enough money put away to consider purchasing a property. She was glad to know that she and Tony were being wise with their money though, and that they were slowly putting away a little more each month.

"One day, Lord. One day," she commented, smiling to herself as she made her way down the road.

Jacqui chattered excitedly with her mother that evening. She mentioned about how disappointing it had been to not be able to ride the day before because of the weather.

"But that was made up for today. God gave us such a beautiful day and Jan took us out on a trail ride for our second ride of the day! Matty was such a good boy in the morning," Jacqui spoke affectionately of her favourite little bay pony.

"That sounds wonderful honey. So Jan took you out on the trail ride?"

"She did! After we'd ridden the ponies that we really wanted to in the morning, she took us out while she rode one of her stallions Red. She said that because we were all riding boys that her stallion would be ok. Apparently he gets distracted by girls, but when it's all boys he settles. It was lots of fun!"

"That's great. So have you had a chance to talk any more with Geordie about God stuff without making Hannah feel uncomfortable?"

"Not at all. But that's ok, Geordie hasn't been asking questions… and I've been praying about it any time I think about it."

"Good girl. I always think that worry is something that people choose to do instead of prayer – and they shouldn't! And please don't be upset if any faith talk upsets Hannah, honey. It's not you that she's getting annoyed with."

"I guess so… so Jan had a new horse arrive yesterday mum. I couldn't see him well because it was raining so much but she took me to meet him today. His name's Jaq."

"Jack! Like our dog?"

"Sort of. But it's spelt J.A.Q."

"Well that's a bit funny, so he has the same name as you then?"

Jacqui laughed in delight.

"I hadn't thought of that!"

"So what's he like?"

"He's gorgeous, mum! Jan says he knows it and that's why he's a bit of a handful. But he's this beautiful tall grey gelding. He's still a pony but he's a lot bigger than little Matty that I love to ride. Jan said that she's working with him to get him a bit quieter before she sells him. She thinks he'll do really well in the show ring because of his looks."

"He sounds like a beauty."

"He is, just like the grey horse I've always dreamed of having. Maybe one day I'll have a horse like Jaq," she dreamed over the phone, causing Kate to smile.

"And what about Matty?" she teased, knowing that Jacqui adored the little bay pony.

"Oh, he's wonderful! I'm just dreaming. I'd be happy with any willing pony that I could ride!"

Kate knew this was the truth. She looked forward to being able to take Jan up on her proposition and to be able to see her daughter riding a pony across their property.

"So I got some papers in the mail that I've been waiting for," Kate commented suddenly.

She'd told Jacqui of her plans to undertake a horse course in the hope that it would generate more customers for them. Jacqui had been excited to hear that it was possible to study horses after school. She was a long way from finishing school, having not yet started high school, but some days she dreamed of running a property like Genesis where she could ride all day and look after other people's horses.

"Was it for your horse course?" Jacqui asked eagerly.

Kate laughed.

"It was! I've signed the papers and sent them back already. I really hope that being able to tell potential clients that I'm studying a horse management course will give them faith in my ability to look after their horses!"

Jacqui agreed that that would be great.

"So you're nearly one week through your stay at Jan's, has it gone by very fast?" Kate asked of her daughter.

"So fast! It'll be nice when Caitlin and Amelia are able to join us and get a few days of riding but then that'll mean that our fun riding time is almost finished. I think I'll be sad then."

"That's understandable darling, but think of how wonderful it'll be when Geordie and Hannah are able to bring their ponies back to Genesis. It'll be so nice to see more ponies content on our property. I wonder if a larger number will give others more confidence in the property, too. The more horses I'm able to say we're looking after, perhaps the more likely others will be to keep their horses here," Kate mused more to herself than her daughter.

Jacqui agreed that it'd be great for her friends to have their ponies closer to home. She was sad to think that she wouldn't be riding with them, however. She kept this thought to herself, not wanting to pressure her mother. She knew that they were being careful with their money and that a lot of it was going into being able to run a property where horses could live.

She wouldn't change that for the world. Even if it meant that she couldn't have a pony for a little while. She decided she would focus her energy on helping her friends look after their horses. Until then, she was going to ride as often as Jan would let her and the other two girls!

After speaking with her father, Jacqui hung up the phone and headed back into the lounge room. Jan had put the air conditioner on and was sitting in a large armchair with a cool glass of juice in her hand.

"That one's for you," she commented, pointing to a glass on the coffee table.

Jacqui thanked Jan and picked it up before sitting beside Geordie on the couch.

"How's your mum?" Hannah asked curiously.

"Good! She's really looking forward to you two bringing your ponies back to Genesis," Jacqui responded, causing the three in the room to smile.

Geordie looked up from the school book that Jacqui had loaned her to read. Jacqui was pleased to note that Geordie was almost halfway through it.

"That'll be awesome! I'm so glad that once we're not here, it doesn't mean that we have to stop riding."

Jacqui nodded, feeling sad again. Hannah nudged Geordie in the side with her elbow. Geordie looked back to Jacqui, realising what she'd said.

"Oh, I'm sorry Jacqui! At least when we're at Genesis you'll get to see the ponies every day and we'll let you ride ours, won't we Hannah?"

Hannah nodded fervently. Jacqui smiled and took a sip of her juice.

"Thank you both! I guess with me being able to ride Kara's horse Banjo and your two ponies at times, I'll still be able to work on my riding skills a lot," she stated, suddenly feeling a little more optimistic.

"It'll be good for you to ride different horses," Jan agreed.

"So mum reminded me about Caitlin and Amelia coming up to visit. Will they be squishing into the room we're staying in?" Jacqui asked Jan curiously.

The older woman smiled.

"I don't think you'd all fit! I was planning to bed them down in the lounge room here. Because this is a bigger room, the five of you can stay out here if you like. It's up to you lot."

The girls started debating what they wanted to do when their two friends came to visit for a few days. They still hadn't made up their minds by the time Jan announced they should be heading off to bed.

That night Jacqui thanked God for the friends that she had who were willing to let her ride their ponies. She thanked Him also for Jan and for the opportunity she'd had to improve her riding skills so much over the past five days.

Even if she didn't have a pony any time soon, she was thankful that she had access to other peoples' horses.

Seven

That weekend the girls were able to take advantage of the weather being warmer again. It was too hot to do much in the afternoons, but they were able to fit two rides in each on Saturday and Sunday before lunch came around.

Jacqui felt a little odd not going to church on Sunday morning, but her mother reminded her over the phone one evening that that didn't mean she had to stop spending time with God. After all, God was everywhere so Jacqui could share every moment with Him.

Whilst Geordie and Hannah were still asleep she read a little of her children's bible, finding out about Noah and the flood in Genesis 7. She vividly pictured the animals being loaded onto the ark, two by two. In her mind, the two horses were a beautiful grey stallion that looked like Jaq and a lovely palomino mare with a deep golden coat and a white mane and tail. She wondered what colour their foals would be.

That morning the girls arrived at the table for breakfast, surprised to find a small pot plant sitting in each of their seats. Jacqui smiled in delight when she realised that it was the sunflower seeds they'd planted the first day they were at Jan's.

"They're growing!" she stated excitedly, looking at each of the three pots.

"Mine has the biggest one in it!" Geordie stated proudly, causing Hannah to laugh.

"My sunflowers still might flower before yours," she challenged her friend.

The girls decided then to plant them next to each other at Genesis so that they could see whose plant would flower first. They discussed a spot in the Kings vegetable garden that they thought would be suitable. Jan laughed as she heard them debating this.

"Just make sure you put them in a spot where they can see the sun," she advised, pulling some cereal boxes out of the cupboard, "now, who's for breakfast?" she asked knowingly.

The girls moved their pot plants aside and started sorting out breakfast while they listened to Jan detail her plans for the day. First they would ride bareback on a horse of their choice and following this; they would tack up the other three ponies and take them out on a trail ride.

Keen to encourage the girls to learn in every riding situation, Jan suggested that they might like to take out a different horse on the trail ride this time. Geordie had commented how much she'd enjoyed riding Patrick on the trail last time and how she thought she might ride him again. This had sparked Jan's comment about riding different horses.

"But I can't ride Rose on the trail, can I?" Geordie asked, pretty sure that she shouldn't take the mare out with Jan's stallion Red.

"I'm sorry but for safety reasons I have to say no. You're welcome to ride Patrick on a trail again, Geordie. But perhaps you'd like to try one of the other boys?"

Geordie thought about this for awhile and then nodded. Jacqui was glad to find that after she and Hannah had discussed who they would ride, Matty was still an option.

"I think I'll take Matty on the trail this time. I don't mind who I ride bareback this morning," Jacqui commented, causing Jan to smile.

"Well I'm glad you three have sorted out which of the boys you'll be riding on our trail ride! What do you think of me packing a lunch and we can stop somewhere and enjoy it?" she suggested, causing Geordie and Hannah to grin at the idea.

Jacqui frowned, wondering what they would do with the ponies while they ate.

"Is something wrong, Jacqui?" Jan asked.

"Well… that sounds wonderful, but what do we do with the ponies?"

Jan smiled.

"It's great that you're thinking about their welfare. Each of my ponies is familiar with being tied up to a stable object. There are plenty of trees on this property that I have tied bailing twine around. We can take along enough head collars and lead ropes with us and place these on our mounts and secure them to a safe tying area. Then we can sit in the shade of some trees and enjoy something to eat and drink. Does that sound ok?"

"That sounds wonderful," Jacqui replied honestly.

"Well then it's settled! How about you three girls go out to get your ponies and give them a brush over while I pack us some lunch? I'll be out shortly to help you finish tacking up and check over the saddles before you hop on."

Needing no further encouragement, the three girls pushed their chairs back from the table and raced outside to grab some halters and lead ropes.

Kate rested her hands around the cool glass of juice she had in front of her. She and Tony were enjoying some time with a couple that they'd met at church a month earlier.

Cindy and Jacob Smith were in their late twenties with three young kids. They'd come into a church service one morning after being encouraged to do so. With a young growing family, the couple were struggling to support themselves and their children. The church that Kate and Tony attended offered hot meals once a week to people in need. This was how Cindy and Jacob had come to know about the church service on a Sunday morning.

Kate had felt for them the first weekend she saw them at church. She'd commented to her husband after hearing about their plight that it would be lovely to be able to invite them over for lunch after church if the opportunity arose.

The weekend prior the Kings had been introduced to the Smiths and this weekend Kate had decided to ask them over for lunch. Cindy and Jacob had seemed unsure, but Kate insisted.

Currently their three young children were racing around the fenced off garden out the back of the King's house. Kate again felt sympathy for the couple as they discussed Jacob's struggle to find a consistent job.

The young man had managed to gain casual work, but based on his age and lack of skill in his current job, he wasn't given many shifts and they weren't very reliable when raising a family was taken into account. To make things that bit harder, Cindy was expecting their fourth child.

Kate thanked God that she and Tony had stable jobs and were able to put away for their future. She vowed then to try and help this couple as much as she could.

Tony and Jacob were discussing the additions that Tony had made to the farm since he and Kate had acquired it. As the conversation got more in depth, Tony invited Jacob outside to look at the round yard that they were discussing. This left Kate and Cindy inside to chatter.

"So when are you due?" Kate asked with a smile, taking a sip from her glass.

"Late May," Cindy replied, her gaze going to her three giggling kids outside.

"Oh! I think I should head out there, they look like they're picking from your veggie garden," Cindy commented in alarm, standing to her feet.

"That's fine! There's plenty there and it's good to see that they like vegetables," Kate joked, standing also.

The pair headed outside, Kate grabbing a bucket as a thought came to her. She headed over to the eldest boy James and handed him the bucket.

"Do you think you and your brother and sister could fill this up with any red tomatoes that you see?" Kate asked him, getting a shy nod in return.

Kate offered Cindy a seat outside while she started picking some silver beet and other bits and pieces from the garden. She placed these into the bucket James was holding. By the time the men had returned, Kate and the three children had managed to fill the bucket with a variety of vegetables and salad material.

"Thank you for helping me with that!" Kate commented, smiling when James offered her the bucket.

"I think you should keep a hold of that bucket, James. Is it too heavy for you to carry back to your parents' car?" she asked, smiling when the young boy shook his head.

"Good."

"But we can't accept that," Cindy protested, preparing to stand.

Her husband rested his hands on her shoulder, keeping her seated.

"Of course you can," Kate stated simply, "think of it as a gift for your whole family. Or rather, a thank you for agreeing to spend some of your afternoon with us. We can get that bucket from you at church next week."

Nodding slowly, Cindy smiled.

"Thank you so much," she responded softly, pulling her youngest up onto her lap as she sought her mother's attention.

The two couples chattered some more outside before the Smiths needed to head home. Kate watched them head slowly down their driveway. Tony watched his wife, smiling.

"I know that look. What are you thinking?" he asked, his arm resting around her shoulder.

"Something that needs some prayer and a lot more thought," Kate responded cryptically, still watching the disappearing car.

She turned to her husband.

"I'm so glad that we're comfortable, even though we're watching what we spend. I love that we have an abundance of home grown food that cuts our costs and that we have a roof over our head and can dream about running such a large property. I wonder... I wonder if we can use this property that God has blessed us with to help others, too."

Tony nodded and chuckled.

"What?" Kate asked curiously, walking down the drive toward their house.

"I'm not sure in what way you're thinking, but I believe if God is prompting both of us, then we'd better not ignore it. Talking with Jacob about the round yard has given me the impression that he knows quite a bit, he's just not been given the opportunity to show it. There are a lot of things around this property that I'd love to do, but work is keeping me fairly busy and I don't want to spend all of our weekends working. What if we were to hire Jacob for a set number of hours each week?" Tony suggested.

Kate grinned.

"Not a lot of hours," Tony cut in quickly, aware that his wife's heart was bigger than their capability to give at times.

"Perhaps we could offer him 5 hours of work each week at a set hourly rate. Then if we find more work and that he's capable, we can increase it. At least then they would have one half day a week that they know they can rely on."

"I love that idea," Kate responded, reaching up to kiss her husband.

"But it's different to what you're thinking?" Tony asked knowingly.

Kate laughed.

"Perhaps my husband, but I think I need to do some research first and work out some figures. Maybe we can focus on providing some work for Jacob first and perhaps we can have a proposal for him by next Sunday."

Tony nodded, in agreement. Kate headed inside to look up community gardens on the computer whilst her husband sought out Ross to play ball outside.

Jan peered in the doorway at the three girls working hard to rub a shine into the saddles. She'd set them on tack cleaning duty for the afternoon. The weather was quite pleasant for summer and so she'd decided they could sit outside in the shed to clean the saddles and bridles.

"So I need one of you to help me out with some gardening. Any volunteers?" she interjected suddenly, smiling at the bored look on Geordie's face.

Her gaze moved to Hannah, who looked like she'd prefer to stay where she was. Her smile continued as she took in Jacqui's eager face. Jacqui looked to Geordie and Hannah before looking back to Jan hopefully.

"Come on Jacqui, I know you like plants and I know these two would love to continue cleaning saddles," she commented with a laugh, causing the other two to sigh in relief.

"Ok!" Jacqui stood up from the saddle she'd been cleaning, following Jan out to the side of the pony paddock.

Jan ducked under the fence rail, stepping in amongst the lucerne trees that Jacqui had excitedly told her mum about. Curious, Jacqui followed her.

"Where on earth are we going?" she asked Jan, having noted that the older woman was carrying a bucket with some gloves, pots and hand shovels.

"Just here!" Jan responded simply, squatting down below some branches of a large lucerne tree.

"I'm glad you were willing to help me, because I think this will benefit the property that your parents have."

"Genesis?" Jacqui questioned, squatting down beside Jan.

"The one and only. I think along with your sunflower plants, it would be a great thing for you to be able to take some of these seedlings home to put in on the property if you think your parents would like that."

"If I think?" Jacqui asked incredulously, "I think that would be wonderful, thanks Jan!"

Jan grinned.

"Well now that's sorted, I think you should help me dig up some of these little ones," she instructed, pointing out some young plants that looked like smaller versions of the lucerne tree they were squatting under.

"Ok!"

Jacqui was so focused on digging up seedlings and putting them into pots that she'd filled with dirt, that for awhile she completely forgot about Geordie and Hannah. It was exciting to think that when she got home, she'd be bringing something for the property with her. Her parents would be happy!

That night Jacqui excitedly told her mother about her day. Kate was rapt to hear about the seedlings that Jacqui would be bringing home with her.

"That's so wonderful, darling. It'll be nice to be able to put some of those trees onto the property. I'm sure they'll be great once they grow bigger," Kate told her daughter.

Jacqui agreed. Kate told her about the visitors they'd had that afternoon after church. Curious, Jacqui asked if any of the children might like to ride.

"You know, I'm not sure. They're fairly young. The oldest boy James is only six. Why do you ask, honey?"

"Maybe when Geordie and Hannah have their ponies on the property we could give them pony rides," Jacqui suggested.

Kate grinned.

"That's a wonderful idea darling, but I think you might want to check with Geordie and Hannah about how they feel, first. The ponies belong to them, after all."

Jacqui agreed, suggesting that it was just an idea.

"And it's a very generous one. Imagine how wonderful it will be when you're able to teach others how to ride in the future," Kate commented, causing Jacqui to sigh.

"I can't wait for that day, mum!" she stated honestly, causing Kate to laugh.

"And it will happen honey. Sometimes we just need to be patient."

Jacqui finished talking with her mum and hung up the phone, heading back out to the lounge room. She smiled when she saw Geordie reading. Her grin widened when she realised it was her bible that Geordie was reading, not the book for school. She prayed right then that both of her friends in the room would want to read their own bibles in the future.

Eight

On the second week that the girls were staying with Hannah's aunt Jan, Amelia and Caitlin arrived. It was a Tuesday afternoon. All five were due to head back home on the Saturday. The three girls got so caught up in the arrival of their other friends that they forgot to be disappointed that their stay was nearing an end.

It was too hot and late in the day for the girls to go for a ride when Caitlin and Amelia arrived, but the other three had already ridden for the day and the two new arrivals were more interested in catching up with their friends, than to be bothered. As Jan had expected, all five decided to crash out in the larger lounge room so that they could share a room and talk late into the night.

Jacqui wondered as she dozed off to sleep, if the five of them were to ride in the morning, which pony would be left out from getting ridden?

The next day dawned bright and early with the heat already prominent. Jan told the girls that the temperature was going to be in the high thirties, so they'd ride once for the day and find something else to do later. Jacqui voiced her concern about one pony not getting exercised, causing Jan to smile.

"You know Jacqui, I think I've got a solution for that!" she stated confidently.

"What?" Jacqui asked curiously.

"How about you girls go and bring the ponies in and tack them up," Jan suggested with a smile.

"Which ones?" Geordie queried.

"All of them," Jan stated simply, shooing them out the door.

With a shrug Geordie headed off to the tack room, the others following their friend. The girls brought in two ponies at a time, Hannah taking one in first with Amelia, then Geordie and Caitlin. Hannah came back to bring in the last two ponies with Jacqui.

The girls quickly brushed their mounts, letting Amelia and Caitlin know about the two that they were riding. Jacqui also told them about Jaq, eager to show them the gorgeous grey pony.

"I'll show him to you after we've finished our ride," she promised the two as she placed a saddle blanket on Matty, checking each side to make sure that it was even.

Jan came out to see how the girls were progressing. After providing Caitlin and Amelia with helmets she stood back to watch their progress.

"Boy am I glad you left one of the taller ponies for me to ride!" she stated suddenly, five pairs of eyes looking at her curiously.

"You're going to ride with us?" Hannah asked in surprise.

"Indeed I am. Do you think I'm too tall?" Jan joked.

She was a short statured woman, not much taller than the girls.

"If you'd left me Matty to ride, I may have thought I was a bit too much for him, but I was pretty sure Jacqui would choose to ride him this morning," she winked at the short blonde.

Jacqui blushed. All five girls continued tacking up, Jan preparing Patrick for herself to ride.

"So are we going on a trail ride?" Geordie asked curiously.

"Maybe. I'd like to see how my two new students go with their mounts, first. I thought we'd start with a follow the leader in the arena. How does that sound?"

"You mean that one person chooses what to do and the others follow?" Caitlin asked.

Jan nodded.

"As long as we're all travelling at a safe distance from each other and you state verbally if you're going to increase or decrease the pace, we'll give that a go!"

For the next half hour the girls did just that, Jan insisting on being on the end of the line. They took it in turns, each girl getting to lead the group on her pony, bending around obstacles, changing direction and increasing the pace to a trot or back to a walk. After they'd all had a go, Jan asked them to line up in the centre of the arena.

She then instructed the girls to have a little canter one at a time. Once they'd done a lap in one direction, Jan told them to come back to a trot, change their direction and diagonal and then try and canter again.

All five of the girls managed this easily, proving to Jan that they were in control of their ponies.

"Ok, trail ride time! We'll head out for a little bit but will be back in time for lunch," she commented, gaining a few cheers from the girls.

Jan held the gate to the arena open, telling Hannah that she could lead the way toward the back paddock of the property. Hannah couldn't have been prouder to do so. Geordie followed her, chattering away about how great Rose was. Jacqui talked over her shoulder to Caitlin and Amelia, asking them what they thought of the two ponies that they were riding.

Once all of the girls were through Jan followed behind, keeping an eye on the five for any signs of trouble. Thankfully the ponies were very familiar with the area and the ride proved to be fun for all involved.

Kate hung up the phone, a huge smile on her face. She sighed happily and thought that Ross and Tony couldn't get home soon enough to share the news with!

The weekend prior she and Tony had gone on a drive to take a look at a couple of older male horses that were for sale. Both were fairly quiet and responsive, but Kate had clicked with the first of the two. He was a large bay standardbred that used to race.

She was thankful to find that he had been a trotter and didn't have any issues with picking up a canter lead, like some ex pacers could. His large stature had been the only thing that had caused her to second guess if he'd be right for the family to ride. Captain as he was affectionately known, was 16.2 hands high.

Tony had later asked Kate in the car why she was so concerned about his height.

"Well it is a long way to fall, honey! I'd hate to think of Jacqui up there – or even Ross – and them taking a tumble."

"Well the long fall to the ground will give them time to think and react," Tony had jokingly responded.

Kate had frowned at his comment, slapping him on the arm.

"Ok, seriously, if he is as reliable and quiet as he seemed when you rode him, then a fall seems less likely to me from him than the other gelding that you rode. Yes he is tall, but if he's going to be quieter to ride than a shorter horse, I would be choosing the taller horse!"

Kate thought it over and nodded, agreeing.

"You're right. I'll ring them tonight about trying Captain out for a week or two."

"Of course I'm right!" Tony had responded cheerfully, causing his wife to laugh.

When Kate had called that night she'd gotten the answering machine. Now a couple of days later the family that were selling Captain had finally gotten back to her. She was delighted to find that he was still for sale and that the current owners were willing to send him out on a trial if Kate gave them the security of a deposit.

Agreeing with this option, it was decided that the Kings would organise the hiring of a horse float and come to pick Captain up on the Friday afternoon. Kate was rapt to think that she'd managed to secure a trial horse in such a short space of time. To make things even better, Captain would have an afternoon and evening to settle before Jacqui got home.

Maybe I'll even have a chance to give him a test ride at Genesis, Kate thought as she headed outside to the veggie garden.

Tony was still at work and wouldn't be home for another couple of hours. Ross was out at a movie with Kara. Kate had given him some money to go but realised that she should talk with Tony about Ross securing a part time job if he was going to get into a habit of going out and spending money with Kara.

Ross would be fifteen that year, the minimum age required to be able to secure a job. Kate thought that as soon as her son was old enough, it would be good for him to learn about earning money and being responsible with it.

It might make him more careful about how he spends money if it's something he's had to earn.

Thinking of finances, her thoughts shifted to the Smith family that they'd had over for lunch the weekend prior. Kate hadn't heard from them since that Sunday afternoon but had consistently found them in her thoughts and prayers. She looked forward to being able to offer Jacob some work when they caught up at church on Sunday.

She was aware that sometimes children didn't get the chance to learn about God or being responsible with work and finances – they weren't taught it by their parents. Although she wasn't sure of either Cindy or Jacob's upbringing, she felt that they were a genuine couple and could really benefit from being given an opportunity to earn and learn.

Kate thanked God that she and Tony had grown up in households where they had been taught about their loving Saviour and how they should respect anything that is given to them. It was important to be a good steward of anything you were blessed with – children included.

Since that Sunday afternoon when the Smiths had visited, Kate had spent a bit of time reading up on community gardens. She'd seen one featured on a gardening show awhile ago and this idea had come to mind after sending some vegetables home with the Smiths. It would be lovely to be able to bless many people with the abundance of their veggie garden.

Kate was aware that it would be even better if she could send Cindy home with some plants to build her own. She wondered if the Smiths had anywhere at home where they could plant a vegetable garden. This led to her questioning if they would be interested in doing so. She laughed as she realised that not everyone enjoyed gardening!

"Still, no harm in asking," she commented to herself as she picked some recently ripened tomatoes.

Kate made a note to check with Cindy when the opportunity arose. She thought how nice it would be to have the whole family over for lunch again one Sunday if they would agree to it.

That night the five girls eagerly discussed their day. Jacqui and the other two were able to bring Amelia and Caitlin up to date on what they'd been doing at Jan's for the past week or so.

The girls were also able to find out from Amelia and Caitlin how their summer Christmas holidays had been. The girls sympathised with Amelia when she mentioned that she and her boyfriend had broken up.

Jacqui thought they were too young to be getting into boys anyway but she kept this thought to herself.

"So are you guys looking forward to being the oldest students at school?" Amelia asked, eager to change the subject.

Hannah nodded. Jacqui shrugged, not sure. She did however state that she enjoyed school, whatever the year level. Geordie groaned.

"I don't want to go back to school ever!" she burst out adamantly, "I think we should just be able to ride ponies every day like we have been here."

Jacqui nodded in agreement.

"Did you know you can study horses?" she asked her friends.

Caitlin voiced that she thought it should be possible, but the others had shaken their heads to indicate that no, they didn't. Jacqui told them about the course that her mother was going to do.

"So your mum's working and studying horses?" Geordie asked in amazement.

Jacqui shrugged.

"I guess so. I know she isn't quitting her job because we need money to be able to run the property. But I think she's doing the course so that we can eventually have more customers at Genesis and this will bring in more money."

"I think study would be much nicer if it was focused on horses... but I don't know about working and studying,

74

that doesn't sound fun at all," Geordie commented, screwing up her face in disgust.

Jacqui laughed.

"What if when mum gets her horse qualification that it leads to more customers at Genesis? Maybe we'll get so many that she could leave her job and be at home with the ponies every day," Jacqui dreamed.

"That would be heaven," Geordie stated after some thought and then, "I guess working and studying would be ok if it led to being at home with horses after a little while."

The girls agreed on this fact. Running a horse property and being able to stay at home each day became the next topic of conversation, the girls all interjecting with what they would have on their dream horse property. It was well into the evening before they settled down to sleep.

Nine

The following morning the girls once again found their sunflower pots sitting on the table where they had breakfast. Geordie's were still growing the fastest. Amelia and Caitlin needed some explanation, before agreeing that it was a great idea to be able to take something home that would remind them of their time at Jan's.

Jan promised the two new visitors that in the afternoon when it was too hot to ride, they would be able to make up a pot of their own to take home. Both girls seemed happy with this option.

The sunflowers were soon forgotten however when it was announced that they should get their ponies tacked up before it became too hot to ride. It was decided that Hannah, Geordie and Jacqui could ride their favourites and Jan would ride the same pony.

She insisted that Amelia and Caitlin switch horses though to be able to try out a different pony and grow their horse riding skills. Both girls agreed to this.

Jan again set up an obstacle course for the five, playing follow the leader through it on her pony. Once she'd gone through once with the girls following, she directed them to go through the course in any order they like, as long as one person led and the others followed.

Jacqui was first to lead and she decided to do the course again the way Jan had. When Hannah took over, she did the course backwards. Geordie had them all following her in every which direction, eager to make as many turns as she could whilst in the lead.

Amelia and Caitlin each took half of the course, and finished it in pairs. This gave Jan an idea.

Putting most of the obstacles off to the side of her arena, she set up a couple of jumps down the long side of the arena. She placed the girls at different ends of the arena and handed Caitlin a stick.

"This is your relay. What you need to do is trot down the left side of the arena and hop over the cross bar. Then when you get to the other end, you need to pass by Geordie's left side and pass it to her so that she can trot back the other way to pass it on. Does that make sense?"

Caitlin nodded eager to get started. The girls practiced a few times each at taking the relay stick handed to them, trotting over a jump and passing it on.

"You girls did wonderfully! I think after all of that racing around we need to give these ponies a good cool out. How about you drop your stirrups and let them walk around the edge of the arena with their heads hanging low. Give them as much rein as they need," she directed them, sitting in the middle on her pony that was half asleep.

The girls did so, sponging down their ponies after the ride. It was getting hot.

Because it was warm and all of the ponies had been worked for the morning, Jan told the girls that that was all they would be doing with regards to riding for the day. The girls were disappointed, but agreed that it wouldn't be fair to expect the ponies to be ridden again in such a short space of time. It would be much too hot later in the day to ride them again.

After they'd sponged them down and put the gear away, they walked back in pairs to put the ponies away in their paddock.

They all laughed as the ponies dropped to the ground to roll once they'd been released. The two greys looked brown once they stood, because of all of the dirt! Jacqui looked at this in wonder.

"You wouldn't know they were grey underneath!" she stated, Caitlin nodding in agreement.

"Someone told me about cream horses being the same as greys on a trail ride I went on once," Amelia commented, "they said their mare would roll any time she was washed and let go, and then would look brown!"

The girls laughed about this, and then headed back to Jan's shed to put their head collars and lead ropes away. On their way back to the house Jacqui made her now usual stop at Jaq's yard to say hello.

The pretty gelding trotted up to the fence, thrusting his nose toward her for a pat.

"Hello pretty boy. I would love it if I could own a pony like you," Jacqui dreamed, smiling as his nose snuffed at her flat palm.

"We could go cantering around Genesis and jump everything in sight. It would be wonderful."

Three of the girls had wandered inside. Caitlin was admiring Jaq with Jacqui.

"Do you think your parents will get a pony for you one day?" Caitlin asked Jacqui.

The small blonde nodded.

"I do! I just know that it's not likely to be soon. Maybe once we have more customers at Genesis they'll be able to look into it for me."

"Maybe by then you'll be confident enough to ride a horse like Jaq," Caitlin suggested, causing Jacqui to smile.

"Oh, I wish! I think Jan would have sold him by then, but I can dream. What about you?" Jacqui asked curiously, thinking that every person should want a pony.

Caitlin shrugged.

"I haven't really asked my parents about it. I like horses but I'm not sure that I want to own one. I'm happy to ride them when I can but don't think it'd be as much fun if I knew I had to do it every day to keep my pony fit."

Jacqui nodded automatically, thinking that surely that was the joy of having a horse – being able to ride it every day! She thought it weird that her main reason for wanting a horse seemed to be her friend's reason for not wanting one. Giving Jaq one last pat Jacqui sighed.

"I guess we should head inside and see what the others are up to," she suggested.

Caitlin agreed, making her way with Jacqui toward the house.

Inside the girls found that the other three were eagerly making spiders to drink. The cool fizzy drinks mixed with ice cream were great refreshment on such a hot day.

Once each girl had a drink they sat down at the dining table to chatter. Jan cleaned up the small mess they'd made whilst they drank.

"I will be calling your parents tonight Geordie and Hannah to make sure they're ready to pick up your ponies after your visit. Do they have access to a horse float at all?" Jan asked as she placed dishes in the sink.

Geordie nodded her head fervently.

"We've been able to borrow one from the East Riding School where we ride. They have a new triple horse float that mum and dad are hiring."

Jan smiled at the information.

"What's a triple horse float?" Jacqui asked curiously, not very familiar with the trailer that was used to transport horses around.

She'd seen them before, particularly when the first clients had arrived at Genesis. Truth be told though, she was more interested in the arrivals than the vehicle they'd arrived in.

"It's a trailer that can fit three horses in it," Geordie responded, Hannah nodding in agreement.

"You can get a single, double and a triple horse float," Hannah added in.

"So what's it called if it can fit four horses?" Amelia asked in curiosity, causing Jan to laugh.

"Then it becomes a truck!" she joked, chuckling at the girls' confused looks.

"Some big horse floats or trucks can fit many horses in them. Most horse owners have a single or a double

80

because they don't have a need to move more than a couple of horses at a time. If a large horse business needs to move a lot of horses, they will often hire a horse truck and driver to come and pick them up."

"So people get paid for driving horses around?" Geordie asked in wonder.

Jan laughed.

"Actually, yes! Some places breed and compete a lot of horses. Often if they need to take a lot to a sale or competition, a truck can be the best way."

"That's what I want to do then when I grow up," Geordie decided suddenly.

"Be a truck driver?" Hannah asked, a hint of disgust in her voice.

"Be a truck driver for horses!" Geordie corrected, large grin lighting up her face.

Jacqui laughed.

"It'd be wonderful to know that you could do things with horses all day for a job."

"Just because you drive horses around doesn't mean you get to spend time with them," Jan corrected, placing the now washed dishes on a rack to dry.

"You may spend most of your day driving, not handling the horses."

Geordie's face fell.

"Oh."

"But there are other horse jobs that you can do to earn money that involves working with them. Maybe you should consider one of these, Geordie," Jan suggested.

Geordie's smile returned. She stated that that was a great idea. This turned into a discussion of what each of the girls would like to do with horses if they could get paid for it.

Jacqui had a chat with her brother Ross that evening. He seemed excited to tell her that his girlfriend Kara was getting a new horse. Jacqui was amazed by this piece of information about their neighbour.

"What type?" she queried her brother, sighing when he responded that he didn't know.

"Where's she getting it from? Is it a boy or girl? Is it tall?" she barraged him with questions.

Ross grumpily told her to slow down.

"I don't know!"

Jacqui paused, thinking.

"So... what do you know?" she asked curiously, hoping the question wouldn't make him grumpier.

"I know that she's getting it in a couple of weeks and that it's younger than Banjo... I think it's six years old. And the cool bit is that she'll let me ride Banjo while she rides the new one," Ross stated proudly, causing Jacqui to smile.

"That's great! And I'm glad she's not getting rid of Banjo."

"Why would she get rid of Banjo?" Ross asked, confused.

Jacqui shrugged. She then smiled at herself when she realised her brother couldn't see this response.

"I don't know," she admitted, "I guess I just thought there wouldn't need to be a reason for one person to have two horses. You can't ride them both at once."

"What about the lady you're visiting? Doesn't she have lots of horses?"

"Well… yes, she does."

"So does she ride them all? Is it important that they all get ridden?" Ross challenged.

"I'm actually not sure," Jacqui replied, thinking this was something she must ask Jan.

"I just know that exercise is good for horses… maybe she has another way of giving them exercise," Jacqui pondered and then after a moment's thought, she spoke again, "Ross, do you have a helmet?"

Her brother laughed.

"I do! I don't think I've seen mum so excited by the idea of having to buy me something. She got one for herself and dad too!"

Jacqui frowned, questioning why her parents would have helmets if they didn't have a horse to ride. She said as much to her brother.

"Maybe they can get some riding lessons with Kara, too," Ross offered casually, causing Jacqui to smile at the idea.

Why not? The two chattered a little more before Jacqui was able to talk with her mum about her latest day and horse ride. After she'd finished she wandered back to the lounge room where the other girls were talking about boys and school.

Jacqui joined in the conversation, more interested in discussing the book they were supposed to have read before the year started. She was pleased to note that Geordie was able to join in the conversation, having more than half finished the book. This confirmed to Jacqui that her friend was indeed serious about keeping the pony her parents had promised her.

Ten

After another ride the following morning, Jan set the girls on tack cleaning duty again. Because of the heat, the five girls sat in front of a fan that Jan had set up for them in the shed.

With the cool air blowing on them they were able to wipe over the leather and synthetic gear with a damp cloth. They then set to work applying saddle soap to the leather pieces of tack. At times the gear got forgotten in amongst their chattering.

"I finished the school book," Geordie spoke up suddenly.

The other four girls looked at her in surprise. Geordie frowned, annoyed.

"What?"

Hannah laughed.

"It's surprising!" she reminded her friend, causing Geordie to smile.

"I guess it is… but I think it feels really good! I'll know what the teacher is talking about because I've already read the whole story."

"Good on you!" Jacqui responded with a proud grin, "I guess I need to finish it so that I'm up to date with you!"

Geordie laughed.

"You bet! Jacqui, now that I've finished the school one that we have to read, do you think I could borrow that horse one you've already finished?" Geordie asked her friend.

Jacqui nodded emphatically.

"Of course!"

The girls continued their chatter, talking of how much they'd enjoyed their time at Hannah's aunt's place. Geordie mentioned again how great it was that the fun didn't have to end once they left. Caitlin pondered this statement.

"Has it been so much fun because you get to ride every day? Or do you think it's because you've been able to ride different horses, learn different things and do jumping, trails, obstacles and other lessons?" she questioned Geordie.

Geordie pondered this and shrugged.

"Isn't that the same thing?"

Jacqui shook her head.

"I don't think so. It'll be great for us all to ride together each day... but one thing I love about being here is that Jan is always teaching us. I've learnt how to ride bareback, how to put a bridle on, how to go around the world on a horse... so many things."

Hannah nodded.

"I guess the fact that Geordie and I can continue lessons at the East Riding School means that we can use the time in between to practice what we learnt in our lesson."

Jacqui nodded, thinking that Kara had said something similar to her shortly after they first met.

"But wouldn't it be great if we could have lessons on a regular basis at Genesis?" she pondered out loud.

Amelia smiled.

"You mean like pony club?" she asked.

Jacqui frowned, unsure. Geordie and Hannah nodded excitedly.

"Exactly!" Hannah replied.

"Ok… can I ask about Pony Club?" Jacqui questioned her friends.

She was informed by the four girls that it was something you did about once a month on your pony.

A group of riders met together at one place and were able to ride dressage in one lesson, games another, theory of the horse and more riding in the form of jumping. Pony club would often run from about 9 in the morning until 3 in the afternoon, with a break for lunch planned in between the four sessions of riding and theory.

Jacqui grinned at the new information. *What a great idea!*

"So who teaches the different bits of riding and theory?" Jacqui asked, wondering how easy it would be to get someone to do so.

Caitlin shrugged.

"I think they're normally horse riding instructors that are qualified," Hannah responded uncertainly, "but I think sometimes it's someone older with a lot of riding experience. I guess it would depend on the people running the club."

Jacqui suddenly thought of Kara. She knew that the older teen was keen to teach others about horse riding. Jacqui wondered if someone who had only been riding for a year was qualified to teach other people about horse riding.

She reminded herself that Kara was the one who first taught her and decided then that the older girl could possibly be qualified to teach beginners.

"Do you think it'd be possible for us to have a Pony Club at Genesis?" she asked of her friends.

Geordie grinned. Hannah shrugged.

"We'd need to have enough people to join in... and we'd need someone to teach us."

"So how many people is enough?" Jacqui asked, causing Caitlin to laugh.

"You're serious about this!"

Jacqui smiled.

"Why not?"

The girls started debating how many people they thought would be enough to run a pony club, if they knew of others who could agist their horses at Jacqui's parents' property and if they felt they would be interested in going to Pony Club once a month.

Jan found the girls still discussing this when she came to tell them that lunch was ready. She smiled at the five surprised faces.

"Well! I guess you've been having fun cleaning tack if you've not realised it's lunch time!" she teased, causing them to laugh.

Jacqui asked Jan over lunch if she knew much about Pony Club and how it was run. Jan answered her questions as best she could, informing the girls that it normally cost to be a member and that it cost to keep a Pony Club running.

"Instructors need to be paid and the grounds need to be maintained," she informed them.

"Grounds?" Amelia asked.

"Absolutely. You need to have a safe area to ride. An arena is best for lessons, whether they're flat work or they involve jumping. Having an open paddock where a group of horses that don't know each other are able to run wild isn't such a good idea!" Jan responded, providing the girls with room for thought.

Geordie giggled as she pictured a group of horses misbehaving, their owners struggling. Hannah asked what she was laughing at. Jacqui looked in alarm at her laughing friend as Geordie explained the picture in her head of horses running away with riders and the accidents that followed.

"That doesn't sound like much fun to me!" she replied, causing Caitlin to nod her head in agreement.

"I don't think Geordie should instruct any lessons," Amelia chimed in, taking their side, "except perhaps maybe theory."

"Just not on horse safety," Caitlin cutting in, causing the three to start giggling.

"Well it seems to me that you all did a wonderful job of cleaning my saddles, so I think that's one theory lesson that any of you could teach quite well!" Jan complimented them.

The girls each nodded in agreement with the statement. Jacqui realised with a start that the idea of teaching others about horses and horse care appealed to her.

She realised that she had a lot more to learn about horses, but daydreamed of a future where there was a busy Pony Club being run at Genesis and she was old enough to teach younger horse crazy students about horse care. Jacqui decided she must remember to talk with her mum that night about looking into the possibility of running a Pony Club. Even if she didn't have a horse to ride, she could join in on the theory lessons!

Jacqui remembered the conversation with her brother the day before about exercising horses and realised she hadn't yet asked Jan. She looked up to where the older woman was collecting plates as the girls had finished eating.

"Jan, how do your ponies normally get their exercise? Do you ride them all yourself?"

Jan laughed.

"I'm a little bit too big for some of them, especially Matty!" she admitted, causing the girls to smile.

"And I'm not sure I'm fit enough to ride them as often as they need to be kept in good physical shape. I know you girls have enjoyed the days when you've been able to ride twice. But I assure you that if you had to ride five or six ponies most days of the week, it is a lot of work!"

Jacqui sat patiently, wondering how Jan kept them fit if she didn't ride them all regularly.

"I have a few different ways of making sure they get exercise. I'm not sure if you've noticed, but their paddock is made up of a couple of hills. They are fed in one area but when they get thirsty, they have to travel up one hill to get a drink. Also, as they spend the day in their paddock eating, they continue to move over these hills. That's a form of exercise for them."

Jacqui pictured the paddock that they'd been picking manure up in earlier in the week. She could visualise the hills but realised with a start that she hadn't noticed them to be particularly important.

"Genesis is quite flat, isn't it?" Hannah asked Jacqui, obviously thinking along the same lines.

Jacqui nodded her head, looking to Jan.

"Is that a bad thing?" she asked.

"Not at all! Besides, the ponies that'll be at Genesis will be owned by people who love to ride and have the time to do so," Jan responded, causing Jacqui's frown to disappear.

"Aside from that, I did tell you that I have a few ways to exercise them, didn't I?"

Geordie nodded, leaning forward on her seat.

"So what are the others?"

"There are times when I go out on a trail ride by myself, but I ride one horse and take another along with me. The second horse doesn't have a saddle or bridle, just a head collar and lead. I'm able to lead them from the horse I ride. This way two get exercise at once."

"I couldn't imagine riding one horse and leading another!" Amelia chimed in, her eyes wide.

Jacqui nodded in agreement. She was glad to find that holding the reins correctly was now a habit for her, but she couldn't picture herself controlling the horse she was riding and another she had to hold onto at the same time.

"Is it difficult?"

"It can be at the start," Jan agreed.

"But any time I have a new horse I start first in the arena. This is done a few times before I consider heading out around the farm or on a trail. That's a reason the ponies are so quiet out on the trail rides that we've been on – they know the area really well."

Hannah smiled.

"I think that's so cool!"

Jan returned her smile.

"It can be hard work sometimes, but mostly it's a lot of fun. The other thing I can do to give them some exercise is lunge them."

Jacqui thought about the act of having a horse move in a circle around its handler, whilst on a lunging rope.

"Do you do that in the arena?" she inquired.

Jan nodded.

"Absolutely. It's enclosed, it's big enough but not too big and the ground is flat."

"So it really isn't impossible if you own more than one horse to make sure it gets the exercise it needs," Jacqui mused.

"As long as you're willing to work for it," Hannah chimed in.

"Absolutely," Jan agreed, "it is a lot of physical work and needs to be planned well. You can't just take a day off because you don't feel like it. But don't think that I exercise all six of those ponies each day. If I can give three or four exercise on a daily basis and give them all a day off on Sunday, that means I can focus on work that needs to be done around the farm."

"You must be busy!" Caitlin commented, thinking this over.

"At the moment you girls are helping me a lot," Jan commented with a smile.

"I know that my ponies are getting all the exercise they need, as well as my stallion Red. Plus I've had time to do things in the garden as well."

That afternoon was a quiet one for the girls. They were thankful that in the heat of the day Jan suggested they sit in front of the air conditioner and enjoy some free time.

Jacqui loaned her horse book to Geordie as promised and planned to focus on the next one in the series. She found her mind wandering though. She thought how wonderful it was that God had allowed her to meet some horsey friends on the first day of her new school in Victoria.

Even more incredible was the chance she'd been given by coming along with Geordie and Hannah to meet Hannah's aunt and ride some ponies. Now she was surprised to realise that although God was blessing her through this time, Jan was also getting blessed by the girls riding her ponies. Jacqui thought this to be the most delightful thing. That evening she discussed this new revelation with her mother.

"He is pretty incredible, isn't He?" Kate asked her daughter, "to know that as well as you getting to learn so much about horses and enjoy riding them, you're also able to bless Jan because of your riding."

Jacqui agreed.

"I hope I can continue to bless people through horses, mum," the young girl admitted.

"I think God gives us desires to be able to carry out His work. Your love of horses is because He put that in you. I'm sure you'll find many opportunities in the future to bless people through something horse related. Thankfully, God will put other opportunities out there for you too. Think of how you and Hannah have worked together to help Geordie with her school work. There are opportunities everywhere you look, you just need to recognise them and do what you can when you can."

Jacqui pondered this conversation as she lay in bed that night. She hadn't realised that God would provide her with so many opportunities to help others. It made her smile to think that even though she hadn't realised God had placed opportunities in front of her to help others, she'd been able to do so without thinking about it.

Eleven

On Friday afternoon the Kings were able to make the necessary trip to pick up their new horse. Ross had decided to stay at home while his parents picked up a float before going on to get Captain.

Now after having picked the horse up, Tony took in his wife's delighted smile and found himself suddenly smiling with her. It felt good to know that they were bringing home a horse that was for all of them. Granted, Captain wouldn't be bringing income to the property, but Tony was aware that the big horse would be bringing other things to the family that were priceless.

To know that his wife would be building up hours in the saddle again, that Jacqui would have the opportunity to learn and exercise and that another horse would make the agistment property look busier were all things that he felt could work to their advantage. Aware that Kate was investing her spare time in study to try and increase their client base; Tony wondered what God had in store for the King family over this next year.

He and Kate were convinced they could afford to offer Jacob Smith half a day's work each week and had considered tasks that they felt were the most pressing at Genesis. Tony was pleased to find that they could think of a few things that would keep the young man busy, whilst also quickly adding to the property's value for customers.

He was also relieved to find that a weight had been lifted from his shoulders. Tony looked forward to spending more of his weekend with his family, rather than working on the property.

Tony slowed the vehicle as they came to the end of their street and rumbled down the drive.

Captain had loaded very sensibly onto the single horse float that the Kings had managed to borrow from Kara's family. He unloaded just as well, Kate still carrying a smile that went from ear to ear.

"This could be your new home, boy!" she told the gelding as she gave him a pat on the neck.

He looked around alertly, nostrils blowing air out softly.

"We'll try you out for a little while and see how you like it here. Eventually you'll be sharing a paddock with others, but for now you've got the house paddock all to yourself so that we can keep an eye on your health," Kate chattered away to him as she led him sedately down the drive to the large paddock located behind their house.

Tony smiled as he watched her go. Ross came up beside him, a soccer ball in his arms and Jack at his heels.

"He's big!" he commented, causing Tony to laugh.

He turned to look at his son.

"Indeed! He seemed a lot quieter than the other horse your mother tried and I think it's better to not fall off a tall horse, than to consistently fall off a smaller one."

It was Ross' turn to laugh.

"Can't argue with that logic!" he responded.

"Of course not," Tony agreed, tapping the ball out of Ross' grasp and running away with it as his son followed in hot pursuit.

Kate was able to open the paddock gate and lead Captain docilely through before closing it after her. She made sure that he was turned to face the gate before she unclipped the lead rope from the head collar.

The mother of two planned to remove the head collar all together before retiring for the evening, but felt it best to leave it on Captain whilst he checked out his new surroundings. This way if she needed to catch him, she would only need to clip up the lead rope again.

The tall brown horse turned around and stepped out into a big trot as he checked out his new home. Kate leant against the gate, thanking God for this new opportunity. She also thanked him for the safety and health of her family and for the fact that her baby girl was coming home the following day.

Her gaze travelled to Tony and Ross playing soccer in the neighbouring paddock, Jake barking and racing after the ball as they kicked it back and forth. Kate smiled.

Looking back to the house paddock, she was glad to see that Captain had settled and was picking at some grass. Opening up the gate, Kate headed toward a little shed that the Kings were hoping to turn into a feed room. Quickly she made up a bucket of some chaff and pellets, mixing them with a bit of water.

This done she headed back out to the house paddock to gain Captain's attention. The gelding's head shot up, his ears pricked as he heard the rattle of the bucket. Kate laughed.

"I guess you like your food then!" she commented as he trotted toward her.

Kate held the bucket firmly as the gelding nudged her in his haste to eat out of the container. She realised with a start that they didn't have any feeders on the property. Although many horse owners would have their own, she questioned if this was something that they should provide for clients who wanted to feed their horses on a regular basis.

Kate was aware that some owners were happy to have their horses at pasture and to provide hay if necessary, but many liked to be able to feed chaff, grains and supplements. She decided to check with Tony to see what he thought. With a smile, Kate questioned if they might be able to source some more tyres from Hannah's father as they'd done for the arena her husband and son had built.

Jacqui couldn't believe how quickly their time at Jan's property had passed. The girls were delighted to find that it was a little cooler on their last full day. This meant they would get to ride twice.

Jan kept the girls particularly busy on their last day, giving them a formal lesson on their mounts in the arena in the morning. After a late morning tea, they packed up a lunch and then headed out on a more sedate trail ride for the afternoon.

It was warm enough for the girls to enjoy the cool water of a creek, their bare legs and feet dangling over the edge, just touching the water as they munched on sandwiches. Jan listened to their chatter as she propped herself up against a broad red gum, enjoying the cool shade it offered.

The group of six returned back to the farm around two in the afternoon. Jan encouraged the girls to untack their horses, give them a good brush over with a curry comb and then to lightly go over the ponies' sweaty spots with a damp sponge.

"They seem most sweaty around the girth," Jacqui commented as she ran the cool sponge behind Prince's left front leg.

This done she moved around to his right side to repeat the procedure.

"You can definitely see where the saddle has been sitting when they sweat," Jan commented, "often it is at the back of the seat of the saddle and their girth area that needs to be washed over to get rid of any dirt or sweat that could dry and cause the horses to get itchy and irritated."

Once the girls had cooled down each of their ponies, they led them out at a safe distance in pairs, releasing them two by two. Jan didn't need to encourage them to put the gear away. It was routine now.

The older woman smiled as they made their way back to her, seemingly unsure.

"Do I sense a question?" she teased, looking at the five.

"Sure! What's next?" Geordie asked, causing Jan to laugh.

"I'm not sure you want to ask that one! But because you have, I'll tell you. It would be a great favour to me if you five would consider taking out the two wheelbarrows to the pony paddock. If you can fill three loads worth like you did last time, it will look a lot better. Plus, it'll be healthier for the grass and the ponies."

Geordie frowned at the suggestion, her motivation improving slightly when Jan mentioned about how it'd help the ponies' health.

"How is it healthier for the ponies?" she queried.

"Horses won't generally eat where there is manure, so even if the grass grows in this area – which it does because there are good nutrients in the manure that encourage grass to grow – they won't touch it. This means there's less grass for them to eat in the paddock, which isn't good. It's better if they have a lot to eat and choose from. Plus, horses can get worms and one way that they can be passed on is through a lot of manure built up in the paddocks."

Hannah screwed up her face.

"I remember being told about that at the East Riding School – yuck!"

"Indeed. Worms in a horse can cause them to get sick, if there are a lot of them. So if you girls are willing, you'll be doing a job that is important and of benefit to the ponies that have given you a lot of fun rides recently."

That was motivation enough for Jacqui. She set off toward the muck heap where the wheelbarrows were found.

The other girls followed quickly, eager to get the job done so that they could say they were looking out for the ponies' health. Plus, the sooner the paddock was picked up, the sooner they could head inside and get a cool drink.

It didn't take the girls long to achieve their task. Geordie commented with relief how much quicker it was because they used two wheelbarrows and had Caitlin's and Amelia's help this time.

"Glad to be of use!" Caitlin responded with a smile, causing Jacqui to laugh.

"It's been wonderful that you two were able to join in at the end, even if you couldn't come for the whole time we were here," she stated truthfully, Hannah and Geordie nodding in agreement.

"Absolutely!" Geordie commented.

"I wonder if Jan has some more tasks in mind for us before we're finished for the day," Hannah pondered as the girls walked out of the paddock, two of them pushing wheelbarrows.

Jacqui looked at the lucerne trees as they walked along the fence line, imagining a time when Genesis would have something similar. She was glad that this daydreaming was a possibility because of the seedlings Jan had given her.

After the girls had emptied the wheelbarrows and put their rakes away they headed back inside the house. Jacqui dawdled behind the others, eager to see Jaq another time.

The young grey gelding was munching on some hay in his yard. When the small blonde approached the fence he lifted his head, eyeing her thoughtfully as he munched.

"You really are the horse of my dreams, do you know that?" Jacqui murmured as he continued to chew.

"I've loved riding little Matty but I hope that when I'm more experienced, I'll be able to ride a horse like you. Maybe Jan would let us come back next year and I could ride you then!"

At the raised voice Jaq walked over to Jacqui, putting his head over the rail to get a closer look at her. Jacqui smiled.

"You are so beautiful," she murmured, reaching up to pat his forehead.

Jaq breathed in deeply, sniffing at Jacqui's hand. She giggled as his warm breath tickled her. As Jaq started to nuzzle her hand with his lips, she carefully retracted it.

"You've tried to nip at me before and Jan's warned me to not encourage you, so that's all the pats you're getting from me for now," she stated firmly.

No longer being patted, Jaq huffed out a sigh and headed back to his pile of hay. Jacqui made her way inside after the other girls.

Jan had already placed a tray of cold drinks on the table and the girls were seated and refreshing themselves. Jacqui took a seat beside them, smiling when Geordie grinned at her.

"Jaq?" she queried, the one word being enough for Jacqui.

"I hadn't seen him today so I thought I'd say hello before heading inside," Jacqui replied.

Geordie nodded.

"It's a pity we can't take him home with our ponies!" she sighed.

Jacqui agreed.

"I'm not so sure about that," Hannah interjected, "Jan's told us what a handful he is. I think it'd be silly to want a horse that is difficult."

Caitlin nodded.

"I don't think Geordie or Jacqui meant they wanted to take home a horse that was a bit much for them, just that he's lovely looking and how nice it would be to be able to have a horse like that."

Jacqui nodded.

"Absolutely! I know Jaq would be too much for me, I'm still so new to horse riding. I wondered though... Hannah, do you think your aunt Jan would consider us making a visit like this again?" she questioned, unsure.

Hannah considered the request, Geordie grinning like a Cheshire cat beside her.

"That's a great idea!" the redhead enthused.

Amelia nodded.

"It's a big ask for someone to take on five girls for a week or two. It's a bigger ask to request that they do it more than once," Caitlin suggested.

Jacqui nodded.

"I guess I was dreaming big," she responded with a shrug.

"I don't think you're dreaming too big," Jan commented, stepping into the kitchen.

The girls jumped, responding as if they'd been caught doing something they shouldn't. Jan laughed.

"I'm sorry. I overheard your conversation and thought I could respond to it without you having to ask me! I'm glad to hear that you'd like to come back for a visit. That tells me that I've done something right!"

"I've loved being here," Jacqui stated truthfully.

The other girls nodded in agreement.

"Good! Well here's a question for you then. You came here to experience some horses, ride and learn and in particular, to find a new home for two ponies. So I have a question for you, do you think Geordie and Hannah that you'd want to come here again and leave your ponies at home whilst you came for a visit for a week or two?"

The girls sat quietly. Jacqui felt sad, realising that maybe another visit wouldn't appeal to her friends if they had to leave their own horses the next time. Hannah mentioned that she wasn't sure. Geordie shrugged.

"I don't see why not. We could give them a break and come up here to learn more and try riding different horses. I think it'd be good for us and wouldn't hurt our ponies."

"Could we bring our ponies with us?" Hannah questioned, causing Jacqui to smile.

Why didn't I think of that?

"Now that's something I'd have to give a bit of thought, Hannah. In a year's time I will no doubt have other ponies that are being prepared for sale. This would mean that Rose and Jasper wouldn't be able to go back into their current paddock. Also, because they will have been on another property with other horses, I need to be careful about their health and how it could affect the horses here."

104

"Oh. How could a different home affect them coming here?" Geordie asked, confused.

"Think about if someone in your family has a cold and they pass it on to you. Then you go to school Geordie and you give it to Jacqui. Then Jacqui goes home and she gives it to her family. A cold isn't really bad, but it's not fun! The same thing could happen to your ponies and then they give it to mine. Or, maybe one of my ponies is sick and gives it to Rose or Jasper."

Geordie nodded, considering the analogy.

"When horses are kept together, it's important to keep an eye on their health as it can affect each of them. When you bring horses from a different area, this could accidently bring a health problem, even if you don't mean to."

The girls nodded as they sat at the kitchen table. Jan sighed at the sullen faces.

"You all look a bit sad! I'm sorry, I didn't mean to upset you, I just wanted you to see what I have to consider about horses coming onto my property. It's what your parents will also have to consider at Genesis, Jacqui."

"There's so much to learn about horses isn't there?" Jacqui asked.

Jan nodded.

"You'll never stop learning! Now, I realise that I've not answered your question even though I've asked you one of my own. It's been a delight having you girls come and visit and help me keep my ponies in shape. I'd be more than happy to have you come and do this again in the future – *if* you want to. But remember, things can change in a year and you may not want to leave your ponies or something else may be more important at the time that you're able to visit."

Geordie shook her head.

"What could be more important?" she asked.

Jan laughed.

"I'll let you know in a year's time if you tell me you can't come for a reason, Geordie," she responded, causing the girls to smile.

Having made a pact with Jan that they would return in a year's time if their parents agreed and Jan was still happy for them to do so, the girls dutifully set to packing up their clothes and other items that had been brought for their stay. All five were getting picked up after lunch. Jan promised that they would be riding once more in the morning, so it was best that they were all packed before that time.

Twelve

Jacqui waved goodbye to Geordie and her parents as they dropped her at the end of the drive to Genesis. It was great to be home!

The young blonde started to race down the drive and then slowed to a walk as she spied trees lining either side of the driveway. She grinned, thinking her parents had been busy. She remembered the trees down Jan's driveway and wondered if this had inspired her parents.

Jacqui smiled as little Magik came up to the fence of the driveway paddock to look at her. Sox was grazing in the centre of the paddock, not at all interested in the lone figure wandering down the driveway.

Sox and Magik were the first two agistees at Genesis. An older retired pony known as Bob had followed shortly after. Jacqui's parents had been leasing the property for just over six months and had been improving it over this time. Kate had always planned to generate an income from the property, but a lot of hard work had had to be put into it before it was safe for horses.

Even once this was achieved; it then needed to be made appealing to horse owners. Many who paid to keep their horses somewhere, also liked to be able to ride their horses on the property.

Jacqui's father and brother had worked hard on creating a round yard where horses could be lunged. Tony had also separated an already standing shed into different bays where horses could be tied up for grooming, feeding or tacking up. The next plan was to develop a safe riding arena.

Tony and Kate were working on this when Jacqui arrived home. She saw her parents walking out distances and putting in markers where the boundary would need to be.

She raced over, eager to see what they were doing exactly. Kate wrapped her daughter up in a hug as soon as she saw her.

"You're home! Did you miss us? Where are your bags?"

Jacqui smiled.

"They're at the end of the driveway along with the lucerne trees and sunflower that Jan gave me. Of course I missed you guys! But I had so much fun, mum and dad."

"I've heard all about it already. As soon as your mum hung up from talking to you each night, she'd give me every detail," Tony replied in an exasperated tone, winking at his daughter.

Jacqui laughed.

"Where's Ross?" she asked of her older brother and then, "Magik and Sox look good."

Kate nodded in agreement.

"Your brother's out in the back paddock walking Jack. The little rascal caught a rabbit yesterday whilst he was off the lead. If you're out walking him in the paddocks, keep him on a lead, Jacqui. I'd hate to think of what could happen if he was so focused on chasing rabbits that he didn't realise he'd run onto one of those busy roads."

Jacqui nodded.

"So what are we going to use to line this arena?" she asked, looking at the tent pegs that Tony had hammered in at certain points.

"We've found a place where we can get railway sleepers cheap. They should be perfect, at least for the longer sides but possibly for the whole arena," Tony commented, looking over the markers that he'd put in.

"And I picked up a set of arena letters at the local saddlery yesterday. So once we get the sleepers in, we can practice dressage and know exactly where the letters are in the arena!" Kate stated triumphantly.

Jacqui smiled.

"We can as soon as we get a horse to ride at Genesis," she corrected her mother.

Kate just smiled.

"I guess you haven't had a chance to look at the whole of the property since you've come home," she stated mysteriously.

Jacqui shook her head, agreeing that she hadn't.

"So I've got a surprise for you. Want to come for a walk?"

Jacqui looked to her father who was trying unsuccessfully to hide a grin behind his hand. Curious, Jacqui nodded and followed her mum as they walked out of the arena paddock and toward the house. What could her mother be up to?

They continued passed the house and to the gate of the house paddock. Jacqui walked through as her mum held the gate ajar for her and then locked it carefully behind. She stopped just inside the paddock and stared in surprise. *We have another agistee!*

A tall bay gelding was standing in the shade of the large trees that were behind their house. It was these trees that had stopped Jacqui from being able to see the horse until she'd entered the paddock.

"You got another agistee!" Jacqui stated in triumph, and then, "he's huge!"

Kate smiled.

"Isn't he? But he's a sweet old man. And the best bit is that he isn't an agistee. He's ours."

Jacqui stared at her mum and then back at the horse.

"Ours?" she asked, incredulous.

"Ours," Kate affirmed.

Mrs. King told her daughter about her search for a reliable horse that the whole family could ride on. She finished by telling Jacqui of how they'd picked him up the day before.

"Ross told me you and dad got helmets! Have you had a ride yet?" Jacqui asked.

Kate nodded.

"Last night. He was really good to take out in this large paddock. I think you'll really enjoy riding him Jacqui."

The young blonde looked at her mother in surprise.

"I get to ride him?"

"Of course! I said he was for the whole family and he's quiet. Just make sure that any time you plan to ride you check with me so that I can be around while you get used to him. I might ride him a couple more times beforehand just to make sure he's really settled here."

Jacqui nodded. Captain headed out from the shade of the trees, curious by the nearby voices. Jacqui held her hand out for him to sniff.

"What are those white marks on his neck mum?" Jacqui asked, seeing some funny lines on his brown coat.

"Captain is a standardbred. That's a brand. That's the way his breed of horse is often identified. I'll have to look up what each symbol means, but I'm pretty sure they represent numbers and the numbers represent the year he was born and in which state of Australia."

Jacqui took in this new information, surprised by it. She thought that she hadn't seen any brands on Jan's horses. She mentioned this to her mother.

"Not all horses are branded but it can be a good way to identify them if they go missing or get stolen. Now that you've seen the family's new horse, do you think we should get your gear and bring it inside?"

Jacqui nodded and followed her mum out of the house paddock to get her gear. It was definitely good to be home.

Over the next week of the school holidays Kate was able to ride Captain a few more times to ascertain that he wouldn't behave unpredictably. Once she was happy she allowed her youngest to have a go.

Jacqui was rapt to be able to rotate between riding the family horse and riding Banjo with Kara next door. This helped to pass the time whilst she waited for Geordie's and Hannah's ponies to arrive the weekend after she returned home. It was Saturday afternoon before they arrived.

Jacqui jumped up and down excitedly as she spied a large horse float coming down their driveway.

"They're here!" she shrieked in excitement.

Dropping the piece of bailing twine she'd been plaiting, she raced towards it, stopping near where she thought the vehicle would get parked. Kate laughed, following her daughter.

The Johnstons had borrowed a float from the East Riding School so that they could pick up the ponies from Jan's place. Geordie and Hannah had been talking excitedly with Jacqui about getting to make the drive from the farm with their ponies. Jacqui had been a little disappointed that an invitation hadn't been extended to her to go with them.

Kate reminded her that with their ponies coming to Genesis, Jacqui would get to see them arrive and see them more often than Geordie or Hannah. Jacqui had agreed, but waited impatiently for her friends to arrive with their new acquisitions.

Kate had had to hide her impatience at the Johnston's arrival. She and Tony had decided to keep the leasing of Matty a surprise for Jacqui. She didn't know yet.

A discussion with the Johnstons about how they were planning to get Hannah's horse to Genesis had brought up the possibility of bringing Matty to the property via the same means. The horse float that they had been able to borrow could comfortably fit three horses. This meant that the three ponies were able to travel down together and not cause any extra expense, which had worked out really well for the Kings.

Geordie and Hannah clambered out of the car as soon as it stopped eager to tell Jacqui about how well the ponies had loaded up at Jan's.

"The adults even let us load them by ourselves!" Hannah stated proudly.

Jacqui thought this was wonderful.

"So does that mean you'll unload them too?" she asked curiously, not having an idea about putting a horse onto or taking one off a float.

"Sure!" Geordie replied, opening the side door of the float to peer in at the ponies.

Mr. Johnston directed Geordie to hop into the float, as her pony would be the first one to get unloaded. Once she called out that she'd untied Rose and was ready, he undid the bolts on the trailer door and lowered the ramp.

Geordie backed Rose out slowly, trying to keep her in the middle of the ramp. The eager pony looked around, calling out as soon as her head was out of the float.

"She's saying hello!" Geordie laughed, causing Jacqui to grin.

Once Rose was safely out of the float and looking around, Hannah got in next. Jasper was a complete gentleman, backing down the float ramp neatly and slowly as Hannah asked him to. The young girl beamed proudly at her brown pony.

"He's so well behaved!" she gushed, patting him on the neck as he lowered his head to snatch at some grass.

While Jacqui was watching the two ponies, Kate entered the float to untie Matty. When she was halfway down the ramp, Jacqui looked over in surprise.

"Who's the third horse?" she asked, before it registered in her mind that she already knew.

"Matty? What's he doing here?" she asked her mum, looking to her father too for an explanation.

Tony smiled at his daughter.

"He's for you, honey. We haven't bought him, but we have arranged with Jan to lease him for you to ride. We hope that's ok," he finished with a grin.

Jacqui looked back to where her mother was holding the pony patiently standing just outside the float. *They got me a pony!*

Taking in both her parent's smiles, she beamed. Quickly Jacqui hugged her father before walking to her mother to do the same. Kate held out the lead rope for her to take her pony.

"Thank you!"

Jacqui looked to Geordie and Hannah, noting their excited smiles.

"Did you both know?" she asked as the three walked toward the arena paddock to put their ponies away.

She just smiled at their fervent nods before stating that she couldn't believe that they'd managed to keep it a secret from her. Hannah admitted that they'd only found out that morning when they'd loaded up three horses instead of two! Jacqui laughed in delight.

"I didn't think you'd be able to keep something like that from me," she teased.

"Too true!" Geordie agreed, turning Rose back to face the gate as she'd been taught to do.

Hannah and Jacqui did the same whilst Kate closed over the gate for them. On the count of three they undid their head collars and stepped back in case their ponies spun around quickly and kicked up their heels.

The three ponies turned around sedately before picking up a high stepping trot, checking out their new home. The three girls stood and watched them for awhile, content.

"How wonderful that we now have seven horses here," Kate commented, leaning against the fence as she watched the ponies pick up a canter.

"Seven!" Hannah turned to look at Jacqui, "that means you haven't told us about another horse here!"

Jacqui grinned.

"So my parents are trialling a horse to buy. I guess you'll want to meet him, huh?" she asked without needing to.

The answer was a resounding yes!

About the Author

Christine Meunier considers herself introduced to the wonderful world of horses at the late age of 13 when her parents agreed to lease a horse for her. She started experiencing horses via books from a young age and continues to do so, but recognises that horses cannot be learnt solely from books.

She has been studying horses from age 16, starting with the Certificate II in Horse Studies. She completed the Bachelor of Equine Science in 2015.

Christine has worked at numerous thoroughbred studs in Australia as well as overseas in Ireland for a breeding season.

She then gained experience in a couple of Melbourne based horse riding schools, instructing at a basic level before heading off overseas again, this time to South Africa to spend hours in the saddle of endurance and trail horses on the Wild Coast.

Particularly passionate about the world of breeding horses, she writes a blog about equine education which you can view at http://equus-blog.com/

You can contact Christine via email at christine@christinemeunierauthor.com.

Sign up to her author news and receive updates – and freebies – as they are available! http://eepurl.com/bAiMpL

Every effort is made to ensure that this book is free of spelling and grammatical errors. That said, I am only human! If you find any errors, I'd love to know so that I can

117

correct them. You can contact me at
christine@christinemeunierauthor.com with details of any
issues you may find.